#2

Slalakum

Glen Sargeant

PublishAmerica
Baltimore

First printing

All characters in this book are fictitious, and any resemblance to real persons, living or dead, is coincidental.

PublishAmerica has allowed this work to remain exactly as the author intended, verbatim, without editorial input.

Hardcover 978-1-4512-3402-2
Softcover 978-1-4512-3403-9
PAperback 978-1-4512-6870-6
PUBLISHED BY PUBLISHAMERICA, LLLP
www.publishamerica.com
Baltimore

This book is dedicated to my wife,
Philadel,
for supporting my story writing

Acknowledgements

I would like to acknowledge the Sto:lo aboriginals of the Northwest Coast for their wealth of beliefs, always with respect for the environment. In borrowing from their mythology, I hope to make kids aware of this.

Slalakum

*Slalakum: a Sto:lo term
used to describe anything unnatural
that might be seen*

Chapter 1

Sleeping in until nine, eating pancakes for breakfast and having the weekend to explore; this was paradise to twelve year old William Katt, better known as Cat to his friends. And to put the icing on the cake, Cat caught a glimpse of the headlines on the front page of the newspaper his dad held in front of him.

"Ghastly Finding—A Body Found Near Spirit Mountain"

"Are you just about done with the paper Dad?"

Mr. Katt peered over top, "You anxious to read the comics?"

"No, I have to come up with a new current events paper for school." Cat never liked to admit his real reason; he liked to keep that secret as long as possible. This looked like a chance to work on a new mystery in Cedarville, something he could add to his "WHY? (Y)—File" caseload. Actually, their Y-files. His best buddy Francis Boudreau II, better known as Frenchie, and Gilda Brockhurst, a girl from his class, made up the investigative team.

"Nice to see you think about school first thing on a Saturday morning. Are you feeling okay," joked Mr. Katt.

"Well I want to take a look at the sports' page, too."

"Now we're talking. Check out those B.C. Lions. In first place."

"Gee whiz, Dad. They've played one whole game."

"Yeah but they won it." They both started laughing.

A few minutes later Cat's mom and dad were off to work leaving him alone with a day of the unknown ahead of him. He gobbled down the last of his breakfast not wanting to waste another precious minute, and grabbed the newspaper.

Ghastly Finding—
A Body Found Near Spirit Mountain
A human corpse was discovered early yesterday morning on a trail at the foot of Spirit Mountain. The body, that of a male in his late 30's, was found by Gus Stephanos who was hiking in the area. The victim's identity is being held back until relatives have been notified. Sergeant MacFarlane would not reveal the cause of death, only to say it was very suspicious and that it appears to be a homicide. They have a suspect they are currently holding.

"Gus found the body! "Sacre bleu," exclaimed Cat. Cat had picked up the odd French saying from Frenchie: sacre bleu, an exclamation meaning zounds or holy cow, was one he liked to use a lot. He rushed to the phone and was about to dial when it began to ring.

"Hello?" Cat asked.

"Hey mon ami. Did you read the paper?"

"I was just going to phone you, Frenchie."

"Woooo, weird! ESP or what?" Frenchie hummed a bar of the Twilight Zone.

"Yeah, and Gus found the body. We need to pay Gus a visit."

Sixty year old, Gus Stephanos was the supervisor of the Cedarville landfill. He was a good friend of the boys. Nearly everyone in Cedarville knew him. He was as well respected and knowledgeable as the mayor himself, despite the connotations of his profession as a mover of garbage.

It took Cat ten minutes to ride his bike over to Frenchie's. Frenchie was in the front yard throwing balls for his dogs Spud and Shep. It seemed incredible that only three months ago the dogs had been part of their "Y" file about missing pets. What an amazing adventure that had been.

As he lay his bike down the two dogs bounded over and jumped all over Cat. He rolled on the grass letting them lick and nuzzle him.

Frenchie ambled over. He was never in too much of a hurry.

"Come on, get your bike. Let's go see Gus," said Cat.

"Ah...I can't. I've got some chores to do. Mom says if I finish all my jobs, at the end of the month I can get a cell phone. One with a built in camera."

"Cool! Think of the evidence that would help us collect," said Cat. Little did he know how important that cell phone would turn out to be.

"Yeah...but I hate scooping up after those two." Spud and Shep sat up; seemingly aware they were being talked about.

"Yeah, and I've got to mow the lawn, and weed the front flower bed."

"Well, the sooner you get done, the sooner we can go."

"Have you looked at my lawn?"

Cat had played in Frenchie's yard numerous times, but he'd never thought about how much work it would be to take care of it. It was huge. You could play a game of volleyball with twelve players and have plenty of room on the sides for spectators.

"You cut all of this?"

"And the back yard."

Cat gulped. "Why doesn't your dad do it?"

"He's out of town meeting some real estate big shots."

Cat felt sorry for Frenchie in a way. Frenchie may have the biggest house in Cedarville, and the best car, but he hardly got to see his dad. In fact, Cat had probably only met Frenchie's dad three or four times since he'd known him. And he'd been best buddies with Frenchie since kindergarten.

"Well, let's get started," offered Cat.

Frenchie's round face broke into a grin like a happy jack-o-lantern. "Do you want to shovel, or mow?"

An hour and a half later, the two boys lay exhausted under a huge birch tree. Shep and Spud sprawled nearby.

"I wonder who that murdered guy was?" wheezed Frenchie. "The paper said it was suspicious."

"One of my favorite words," crooned Cat. "Come on. Let's go."

"Oh. Man. Can't we just lie around for a while? We just worked our butts off."

Cat leaned over and smacked Frenchie on the rear. "Some of us still need more work."

"Hey." Frenchie punched Cat's shoulder.

"Let's ride over to Gilda's and see if she wants to come along."

Frenchie told his mom they were off to Cat's house and would be back for supper. Stretching the truth was something Frenchie had learned to do when he was on a case. They were off towards Cat's house, it's just they would be making slight detours on the way. "Take the dogs, and don't be getting into any mischief," said Mrs. Boudreau.

That was like telling a dog not to pee on a fire hydrant, thought Cat. The "Y" files involved mystery. Mystery and mischief went together hand-in-hand.

Riding north along Cedar Drive, they passed over the railway crossing and soon were in sight of the Beaton's old farm house. The 'For Sale' sign stuck in the front yard was the newest improvement to be added to the farm in years, maybe centuries. But it too was beginning to rust and lean over. Like the property was haunted or something.

"Good luck selling that place," said Cat.

"Yeah I still get the creeps," answered Frenchie.

Five minutes later Shep and Spud barked a friendly greeting to Gilda's dog, Chester, waiting at the end of her gravel driveway. Gilda lived in an old farm house further out of town along Cedar drive. The three canines chased each other in circles while Cat and Frenchie knocked at the front door. They were totally shocked at their greeting.

Long waves of thick blonde hair fell to her heaving narrow shoulders. Stray locks hid half of her face. Tears flowed steadily from her sad eyes.

"Are you alright?" asked Cat. Cat was worried her dad had done something. Gilda's dad had a history of being drunk and mean. He was not a man you wanted to tamper with.

Gilda hung her head. "My dad is in jail. He is being held for the murder of a man he worked with."

Frenchie and Cat looked at each other and both whispered," Sacre bleu."

Chapter 2

As Gilda was too upset, they didn't think it a good time to ask her along. So with Spud and Shep leading the way, the boys rode their bikes back to the railway track. This was the faster way to reach the dump, rather than going back towards Cedarville. And it was much more open to adventure.

As usual, Frenchie bounced along twenty feet behind Cat. "Hey, Cat. Can we have something to eat now?"

"Let's wait until we're over the bridge," shouted Cat.

"What's the hurry," puffed Frenchie.

"I think the train is due any time," smiled Cat. "We don't want to be on the bridge when it passes over."

"What do you mean the train is due?" Frenchie pushed harder on the pedals. "You didn't tell me the train was coming now." He pumped his legs harder until he was just a few feet behind Cat. He might have too many milkshakes around his middle, but he had strong legs. He'd never lost an Indian leg fight with Cat.

Halfway across the railway bridge, Frenchie made the mistake of looking down. Through the railway ties fifty feet below, the dirty Thuwelman River carried its spring melt water, so the water was high and rising. If they were to get any rain, there could be a danger of flooding. A train whistle blew off in the distance.

"Come on Frenchie, shake a leg."

"I'm shaking more than that," moaned Frenchie.

The train whistle blew again, sounding much closer.

"Don't look down," yelled Cat.

Too late for that, thought Frenchie. He was three quarters of the way across, when he saw the train. It was about a hundred feet away, coming directly at him. His mind froze, but fortunately his feet kept moving. Too bad his feet couldn't keep pace with his heart. If that was possible he'd be at the dump by now.

Cat pulled off the tracks to the side hill. The train engineer must have seen them because he blew the whistle again. "Come on Frenchie, you can do it."

Frenchie wanted to jump off his bike and run, but he knew that would be even slower. He buried his head in his shoulders and pedaled like his life depended on it. He thought he could smell diesel fumes. Geez it must be close. His bike vibrated as the rails and ties sensed the heavy beast approaching. When his front tire hit solid ground, Frenchie lost his balance and slid with his bike down the slope. Through a cloud of dust, he saw Cat's smile, as above him the train rumbled across the trestle bridge.

The boys drank water from their bottles, watching the long freight train click-clack by. When it had gone Frenchie's face changed from the victory smile to a frown. "Are you trying to get me killed, mon ami?"

Cat glanced at his watch. "According to my watch, the train isn't due for another half hour. My watch must be slow. But not as slow as you," he teased.

Frenchie gave him a fake punch to the face. Suddenly he froze. Where are the dogs? In all the commotion he'd forgotten about the dogs.

As if reading his mind Cat said, "Hey, where are your mutts?" Quickly they rode back to the top of the tracks to get a better view. In front of them the tracks hugged the river on the left, and the forest sharply ascended Spirit Mountain directly ahead. Off to the right was a narrow trail that also followed the bank of Thuwelman River that eventually came to the landfill site. Mounting their bikes they took off down the trail. They'd ridden about half a kilometer with still no sign of the dogs, when Cat pulled to a stop. Frenchie squeezed around him and kept pedaling. "Here Spud. Shep, come here boy!"

"Missing pets?" thought Cat. No. No way. He took off after Frenchie.

Frenchie's bike bounced off tree roots and he was whipped in the face by some low evergreen branches, but eventually he came out on the broad meadow that was the landfill site. In the distance he could see smoke and hear Gus' small bulldozer rumbling. And then over a gravel hill came Spud and Shep, chasing a rabbit. The rabbit zigzagged crazily and then disappeared into a hole. The dogs circled the spot then began to dig.

"Oh the mighty hunters," laughed Cat pulling up beside Frenchie.

"More like hound dogs."

Cat and Frenchie broke into a chorus of Elvis Presley's song 'Hound Dog'. "Oh you ain't nothin' but a hound dog, crying all the time. You ain't never caught a rabbit and you ain't no friend of mine."

After giving the dogs heck for running off, to which they wagged their tails in oblivious misunderstanding, the boys rode over to visit Gus.

Gus turned off the machine and gingerly climbed down. His old legs stiff and wobbly like a new born fawn, he stopped and let the circling two dogs smell him. He pulled out a handkerchief from his pocket to wipe his brow and the back of his neck. "Hey, boys. Where you been hiding?"

"At school," groaned Cat.

Gus leaned over to pet the dogs. "Well one more month of that and you'll have all summer to get into trouble," he chuckled.

"Speaking of trouble," said Frenchie," we heard you found a dead guy."

Gus stood. His weathered smile disappeared into shadows of concern, maybe even fear. "Boys, you never want to see what I saw."

"The paper said it was a man who was killed, but they didn't release any details except that it was suspicious," said Cat.

Gus snorted, "Suspicious. Now that's an understatement."

"Under...what? Asked Frenchie.

"Understatement. A statement that covers less than the truth or fact," explained Cat. "So what were the facts, Gus?"

Gus hung his head and whistled. Shep and Spud's ears lifted. They sat looking at Gus, as if they too were anxious to hear Gus' story. "Well, tell you what boys. It's about time for my coffee break so let's sit and have a snack."

Frenchie's ears perked up. "Yeah, snack time. I'm starving." During all the commotion he'd forgotten about food.

Gus had some large, round pieces of log set up as "stump chairs" where they sat and pulled out sandwiches and water bottles. The dogs meanwhile lay down waiting for any stray bits that might come their way.

Gus started his tale. "I was hiking up the trail from the lake at the foot of Spirit Mountain...you boys know where I live, coming here to work. It usually takes me about forty-five minutes. I had only started out when I heard them crows. Those birds are always flying about this place digging through the garbage. But they're not usually so close to my cabin on the lake. I watched several of them hover and then fly down just off the trail. Well they peaked my interest, thinking they may have found a deer or moose carcass. There was a spot where the weeds and shrubs had been trampled down leading to the crows. So I stepped off the trail and followed the worn path until I came to a big old cedar. That's where I saw him."

Cat's eyes were as big as saucers, "You saw the dead man there?"

Gus nodded. "I was scared so I ran home and phoned the police."

Cat couldn't believe Gus would get scared of a human corpse. He'd told the boys about serving in the Korean war where he'd seen many men die. So why was Gus so scared this time? Yet he was too embarrassed to ask.

"Why were you scared?" asked Frenchie. Leave it to Frenchie to not hold back.

Gus puffed his cheeks and blew out a breath, pausing to find the right words. "Well...what I saw... made no sense. Firstly the crows were there all right. But they weren't pecking at the body like they normally do with dead carcasses they find. They flew away the minute they saw me. Then I saw him." Gus swallowed," The man was white. Ghostly white, his eyes wide, and his mouth open, as if he were screaming."

"He must have been afraid of the person who killed him," whispered Frenchie.

"But that's not all," said Gus.

The boys stood closer together.

"The man was hanging upside down from a branch, ten feet up the tree. His legs were tied with some kind of vine."

Chapter 3

Gilda pondered the bright, yellow dandelion poking between the tomato bushes. Now what makes you different from the tangled tomato vines? She touched its soft petals. You're just trying to fit in. I know what that's like. She reached in, sighed, grabbed the dandelion at its base and gently pulled it out. Sorry, but sometimes life doesn't work out the way you want. She threw it on the growing pile in her wheelbarrow.

The sun inched over Spirit Mountain as she walked the rows of vegetables seeking other growing intruders. She didn't mind this chore. There were worse jobs. Like shoveling the stalls in the barn. That would be on tomorrow's list after church. Would they be going to church? Her dad wouldn't be that's for sure. He was in jail.

This was no surprise to Gilda, her dad had been in jail several times for drinking and fighting. But since the incident last year when Gilda had been kidnapped by that awful Beaton family, but escaped unharmed, her dad had not been drunk once. At least as far as Gilda knew. In fact her dad had got temporary work at the cedar shake mill. He'd purchased a cow and half dozen chickens in order to get the small farm running. And he had devoted time to making them a happy family again. She now looked forward to when he came home from work. To have him help with her homework. Or take her hiking and fishing.

Gilda's mother was much happier. Gilda had heard her singing while cooking or sewing or cleaning or doing any of the house work. Her mother had a good voice. She'd been in a small band when she'd met Gilda's father. She was singing at a town dance when he had ditched his date to get to know her.

But now this thing had to happen. Why did he have to go and mess it up? Why once they were on the right track again did he have to make her doubt him all over again? Gilda wasn't sure what had happened, only that a man had been killed and they said her father did it. Gilda's heart felt like a hard packed snowball that would continue to slowly shrink and finally melt completely if things didn't get better.

"Gilda? You just about done out there?" her mom called.

"Coming, mom."

Gilda's lip quivered as she looked into her mom's sad, red eyes.

"Put on your nice dress for your father, okay?"

Gilda nodded. "Is dad coming home?"

"No, honey. We just get to visit."

Due to the seriousness of the case, Mr. Brockhurst had been transferred from the Cedarville jail to the Vancouver prison. The drive to Vancouver took an hour. Normally Gilda loved to visit the big city. But today the tall buildings and bright, billboards were like the wallpaper in her room, unimportant and common.

Mrs. Brockhurst parked her rusting Toyota Corolla in the visitors' parking area of the Vancouver prison. She held Gilda's hand as they walked up the sidewalk to the front doors. As they entered, her mom gave her hand a little squeeze.

After checking through security, they were escorted to a room down the hall. Everything seemed so quiet, nothing like the police stations on TV shows. Gilda, wide eyed and nervous, was surprised. The room was just like any room with carpets, tables and chairs and even pictures on the walls. Except the pictures were of men holding big fish or standing beside dead animals they'd shot.

"Hi, honey," said her dad rising out of his chair and hugging her mom. They held each other for a while before he bent down and wrapped strong arms around Gilda.

"How's my girl?"

"Fine," she stated. Inside Gilda was quivering with a mixture of emotions. But outside she had learned to show nothing. She could not depend on her father's behaviour.

"How's Bessie and Tillie? You milking them regularly?"

Gilda nodded, then stepped back. "What did you do, dad?"

The silence in the room lasted an eternity. Finally Mr. Brockhurst said, "Come sit down," as he extended his hand towards Gilda. But she reached out and clutched her mom's hand instead.

They sat down with Mr. Brockhurst on one side of the table and them on the other. Mr. Brockhurst sucked in a huge breath and started telling his story.

"Fred and I went fishing, right Ellie?"

Mrs. Brockhurst nodded.

"But why did you take your rifle?" asked Gilda.

"Well...yeah...I did. Wait, just let me tell it. I always take my rifle. Never know when a bear might pop up."

"Out in the lake?" asked Gilda. Mr. Brockhurst's eyes darkened.

"Let dad explain, Gilda, be quiet," said Ellie Brockhurst.

"Anyways, Fred said he caught one and started reeling it in. He was reeling and spitting tobacco juice out the boat at the same time."

Gilda scowled.

"Yeah, I know. Fred is kinda gross that way." Mr. Brockhurst hung his head. "I mean he used to be." Silence ticked off the clock as a tear popped out of Mr. Brockhurst's eye. He looked up. "Then

27

suddenly Fred stopped reeling and stood up. He reached down into the middle of the boat and grabbed my rifle. I said, "Fred, what the hell are you doing?" Next thing I know, he's firing into the water screaming, "Holy crap..." Then I don't know how, but the boat lifts up. I fall backwards and hit my head on the gunwale. I black out. When I wake up I'm in the boat floating in the middle of the lake. Alone. Fred is nowhere in sight. There is blood on his seat. I quickly fire up the motor and drive all over the lake looking. I must have spent a couple of hours." Mr. Brockhurst shakes his head as more tears fall. "But I couldn't find him." He let out a big breath. "Ellie, I didn't do this. Why would I shoot Fred? Somehow the boat tipped and he must have fell in and drowned. It was an accident."

Ellie nodded and reached out to hug him when the guard came and announced time was up. He reached out for Gilda, and she responded, holding him tight.

"I believe you dad."

Chapter 4

Sunday morning Cat was awakened by his dad. He'd had trouble getting to sleep. Gus' story had provided enough images to give him nightmares.

"You want to go up to the lake, today? Catch us some supper?" asked Mr. Katt.

Cat sat up and rubbed the sleep from his eyes. "Uh, sure dad. Can Frenchie come along?"

"Only if he keeps his line away from mine," chuckled Mr. Katt.

"Dad, Frenchie got mixed up. He didn't mean to," said Cat. The last time Frenchie went fishing with Cat and his dad in the boat, he'd been sitting in the back trolling when Mr. Katt felt his line being pulled. Thinking he had a fish, Mr. Katt began reeling in, when Frenchie who was sitting in the middle of the boat, felt his line pulling. "I've got one, "yelled Frenchie. Frenchie turned the handle and pulled back on his fishing rod. When he did, his line got stiff and his rod bent. Mr. Katt's line suddenly pulled down so he reeled harder and pulled more, causing Frenchie's line to pull down. It was just then that Mr. Katt figured it out, but not before Frenchie used all of his strength and pulled. Suddenly Mr. Katt's rod flew out of his hand.

"I've got it," screamed Frenchie as he felt the pressure on his line lessen.

"I hope so," said Mr. Katt.

Frenchie reeled until his catch came out of the water. Mr. Katt's fishing rod dangled at the end of Frenchie's line. Cat bellowed with laughter. Frenchie sheepishly looked towards Mr. Katt who was also laughing until tears came into his eyes.

After a quick breakfast, Cat helped his dad lift the canoe onto the rack on top of the aging Ford F-150. Cat put the fishing rods and tackle boxes in the back as Mr. Katt tied the canoe down. Mrs. Katt had declined an invitation to join them, saying she needed to catch up on her reading. But she packed them a lunch and wished them luck.

Frenchie and his mom met them on their driveway just as Mr. Katt turned the truck off. The dogs greeted them with barks and wiggling behinds.

"You guys have to stay home today," said Frenchie.

"Francis do you have your jacket?" asked Mrs. Boudreau.

"Yes, mom."

"And do you have your hat?"

"Yes, mom."

"Do you need gloves? Earmuffs?"

"Mom, I'm not going ice-fishing. I have everything in here," Frenchie said holding up his pack.

"No you don't," she said. She held up a large paper bag. "I know you will need a lunch." She kissed him on the cheek and Frenchie's face reddened. "You be careful, "she reminded him for the umpteenth time and stuffed the lunch in his pack.

As Mr. Katt drove down the driveway he asked," Has your mom ever been fishing?"

Frenchie looked at him, and rolled his eyes. "Uh...no. The nearest my mom would get to a fish is in a can at the grocery store."

"So I take it she won't be cleaning any fish you catch."

"Only if she can use the vacuum cleaner." They all laughed.

Driving north along Cedar Drive, they crossed the railway tracks and soon spotted the boarded up house and and overgrown yard with a real estate sign advertising the place for sale. Only it had a big SOLD sticker on it.

"Someone must have bought the Beatons' place," said Mr. Katt.

Cat and Frenchie stared in disbelief. "Who'd want to buy that place?" said Cat.

"Well, seems like someone did. Actually a coat of paint and some yard work the house wouldn't be too bad. That barn though I think is a lost cause. A strong wind could blow it down."

When they passed Gilda's house, Cat wondered what was happening with her dad. How was he mixed up in the death of that man Gus found?

Twenty minutes later, Mr. Katt was untying the canoe and the boys were dipping their hands in the water. The gravel boat launch was already busy with other boaters getting ready for a Sunday of fishing. Mr. Katt carried the canoe on his shoulders and gently eased it upright onto the closest bank. "Hey you guys going swimming or fishing?"

The boys stopped trying to splash each other and loaded the fishing gear and their packs into the canoe. When Mr. Katt had loaded his stuff, Cat sat in the bow and Frenchie in the middle. "How about you guys trade places."

Cat looked at his dad. "Oh...right." Frenchie shrugged sheepishly, and they traded spots.

Mr. Katt pushed off and in minutes they were moving towards the middle of Cultus Lake. The spot where the fish were, according to Gus, the long time resident of the lake. The spot where last time Frenchie had caught a fishing rod.

When they reached their "fishing hole", they attached the flies to the ends of their lines. Mr. Katt waited for Frenchie to cast his line way out the front of the canoe, and then he tossed his way out back. Cat heaved his line. "Hey Frenchie, I'm on the port side."

Frenchie started to turn his body to talk with Cat. His line naturally shifted coming around the same side as Cat. "No, Frenchie. Keep your line at the bow." Frenchie quickly turned back.

Mr. Katt laughed. "That's right sailors. Stand your stations. That doesn't mean stand up," he quickly added. "Actually do you know the port side used to be called the larboard side but it sounded too much like starboard? So they changed it to port, the side next to the dock where ships were loaded. And also..."

Frenchie was not paying attention anymore. There was something near his line, where it went into the water. He let go of one hand to adjust his glasses. Was that a fish? It looked too dark for a fish. It looked too fat. Was that black hair?

His stomach rolled and he suddenly felt very queasy. His face felt hot. He swung his line, dropped his rod in the canoe, leaned over the edge and vomited.

"Geez, Louise, "said Cat. "Are you alright, Frenchie?"

Mr. Katt looked over his shoulder. "You okay, son? "

Frenchie shook his head as another spasm turned his stomach inside out and he added more of his breakfast to the lake.

"A touch of motion sickness, maybe?"

Frenchie keeled over inside the canoe.

Chapter 5

Cat shoved his rod under the gunwale and leaned down to his fallen friend. Frenchie's glasses hung askew, his eyes closed. But his steady breathing ensured Cat he was okay. Well at least, alive. He cradled Frenchie's head in his lap.

"He passed out, dad."

Mr. Katt reeled in, placed his rod inside and picked up the paddle. "We'll take him over to Gus' place, it's the closest spot," he said, as he aimed the canoe for the cabins off in the distance.

Fifteen minutes later, Mr. Katt steered the canoe to a wooden pier stretching into the water like a lizard's tongue seeking a drink. He climbed out onto the dock and pulled the canoe by a rope attached to the bow. He was pulling it up the beach when Frenchie stirred.

"Fur," said Frenchie, his eyes looking up at Cat.

"Dad, he's coming to," announced Cat.

"Fur," said Frenchie lifting his head.

"Fur?" asked Cat.

Frenchie nodded, "Fur."

"What the heck are you talking about?"

Mr. Katt helped Cat get Frenchie out of the canoe. "How are you doing, Francis?"

"I'm okay now, Mr. Katt. I don't know what happened to me?" Frenchie was about to tell them what he saw in the water when a loud voice welcomed them, "Hello strangers."

Gus stood on the porch of his cabin. Moss clung to the roof of the A-frame structure whose grey cedar walls contrasted with the deep green evergreen forest behind it. Once everyone was inside Mr. Katt explained, "One of my crew got "seasick" on these treacherous waters."

Gus chuckled, "Blimey, bin 'ere meself on occasion," he said in his best English accent. "Care for a coffee? How about a root beer boys?"

After serving the drinks, Gus and Mr. Katt began talking "adult stuff", politics and sports. Cat and Frenchie wandered outside.

Cat picked up a flat stone and threw it out across the smooth, clear water. "Five skips," he said.

Frenchie tried his luck. His rock was larger in diameter, but not quite as flat. They watched and counted together," One...two...three...four."

Before his next throw Cat asked," So what happened out there?"

Frenchie tossed a six. "All right, beat you." He waited for Cat's turn. Cat put his hands on his hips.

"I...I'm not sure. It was weird. I was fishing and then I saw...I saw all this black fur under the canoe."

"Black fur?"

"Yeah." Frenchie tossed another rock high in the air as far as he could.

"Are you sure it was fur? Maybe it was weeds. This lake has a lot of weeds. "

"Yeah I know, but out that deep?"

"Or maybe just a piece of driftwood?"

"Yeah, I guess. But what made me sick all of a sudden?"

"Like my dad said, you probably just got disoriented when you were looking down."

Frenchie shrugged. "I guess."

"Hey let's go dig up some worms for bait."

They found an empty can and shovel under Gus's porch storage area. Frenchie followed Cat around the back of the cabin to a trail that tunneled through cedar trees towards Spirit Mountain. A few feet off the trail there was an enormous cedar tree; Cat and Frenchie would just barely be able to join their hands around it if they tried. Here they dug up the black soil in search of worms. But they found nothing.

"It's too dry here, said Cat. "Worms need moisture." He pointed to a patch of moss about twenty feet further off the trail. Frenchie had to duck when a low branch Cat moved nearly knocked him down.

"Hey, watch out."

"Keep your eyes open, Ke-mo-sah-bee."

"What is that anyways?"

"You never seen the Lone Ranger?"

"Is he a Power Ranger?"

"No," chuckled Cat. "No, it's from an old TV western. My dad sometimes watches it with me. He says he used to watch it when he was a kid. The Lone ranger was a Texas Ranger who had an Indian friend named Tonto. Tonto often called the Lone ranger Ke-mo-sah-bee which meant 'faithful friend' in his native language."

"Vous etes estrange."

"What's that mean Ke-mo-sah-bee?"

"It means you are weird in my native language."

Cat dug under the moss and found some long, reddish pink worms that he threw in the can. A sly grin twisted his face. He threw one that landed on Frenchie's neck.

"Uh...gross," yelled Frenchie, quickly brushing it off. "Cut it out."

"Hey put it in the can," said Cat.

Frenchie's face soured, his nose wrinkling up. He reached for the worm, but when it started slithering he pulled back his hand.

"Come on Frenchie, it won't bite you.

Frenchie picked up a short stick, hooked the wriggler with it and dropped it in the can. In the midst of their worm mission, they had not really paid much attention to the birds chirping and squirrels chattering. But when it suddenly got very quiet, they noticed the change. Cat stopped digging and looked around.

"What?" asked Frenchie.

"Sh...sh...sh."

Somewhere a dry branch snapped. Bushes rustled. Something was coming through the forest. Cat and Frenchie froze, statues except for widening eyes. Frenchie saw it first. He wondered if he would be sick again.

"Fur," he whispered. "Black fur."

Chapter 6

Frenchie's feet could not move fast enough. If they gave out ribbons for speed where fear is the motivation, Frenchie would win gold. He stormed past Cat towards the trail. In the process, he knocked over the can of worms.

Cat turned to follow, but his foot caught a root. Instinctively, he threw out his hands, but he fell awkwardly onto his stomach, narrowly missing some sharp branches. As he rolled over he couldn't breathe. He'd winded himself. A snuffling noise preceded by a large shadow covered his prone body.

Frenchie didn't stop until he reached the clearing. Only then did he notice Cat wasn't behind him. Wiping sweat off his face, he yelled," Cat!" He doubled over trying to slow his racing heart. "Cat?" he yelled again. Where was Cat? What was going on? Should he run for help? Geez Louise.

Seconds turned to minutes when he finally heard Cat's call. "Hey Frenchie, come on back. You've gotta see this."

"What? Are you okay?"

"Yeah. Come on, check this out."

Frenchie hesitantly crept back to the spot he'd just fled. What he saw made his eyes widen, but also a big smile creased his face. A black ball of fur was sitting on Cat's chest. It was making squealing noises while a long pink tongue licked Cat's face.

Cat protectively moved his hands in front the tongue's snakelike twisting. "Okay little guy. Enough with the face wash already." As he sat up the black bear cub lifted his face, sniffing at Frenchie.

"I don't believe it Frenchie. But I think this is the same bear cub I ran into when the Beatons killed her mother."

Frenchie gazed into the forest from where the cub had emerged, as if he expected to see something else come out too. He was sure when they first spotted the black fur, it was much larger. Also now the birds were chirping again. "What's she doing back?'

"I don't have the foggiest idea. Hey what are you looking for?"

"I don't know. But I thought I saw something bigger..."

"Hey, boys? Where are you guys?" As Cat's dad's voice filtered through the trees, the cub quickly scooted out of sight.

"We're coming dad." Cat took one last look to where his furry friend had escaped. "Come on Frenchie, we'd better get going."

When they got back to the cabin, Mr. Katt and Gus were standing at the edge of the lake.

"Don't tell them about the cub, Frenchie," Cat uttered quietly.

"Okay." replied Frenchie. He had stopped and was staring at the waves lapping up the beach. As they receded he felt like they were pulling him. Pulling him out to the deep blue water. To the black furry thing that was waiting for him.

"What's the matter, Frenchie?

"I don't want to ride in the boat."

Cat saw the pale look on his friend's face. He looked out at the lake. "Oh, I get it. Uh...well..."

"Hey, boys. Where you been?" asked Mr. Katt, walking with Gus to meet them.

"Uh... we were looking for worms," said Cat.

"Did you get some?" asked Gus.

Cat was trying to figure out how to help Frenchie. He made eye contact with his friend. "Yeah," he replied, forgetting the can had been knocked over in the melee.

"Where you hiding them?" asked Mr. Katt.

"Oh, yeah. Well we let them go."

Mr. Katt's face scrunched into perplexity and he looked at Gus.

"Save the worms?" joked Gus.

Cat blushed and finally thought he should just come out with it. That would be the easiest. "Dad Frenchie doesn't want to ride in the boat."

Now Frenchie blushed and pushed Cat on the shoulder.

"Alright. Uh...not feeling like you can stomach the ride, son?"

Frenchie looked at his feet.

"Well we've got to get you home somehow."

Gus could see Frenchie looked paranoid about getting back into that boat. "You know what? I could drive you back home, if it would make you feel better."

Frenchie's face brightened.

"Seems like an inconvenience, Gus," prompted Mr. Katt.

"No, I don't mind. Actually wanted to go the store for some things anyways."

"Can Cat come too?"

"Sure. Come on boys. Jump in the truck." Gus winked at Mr. Katt. "You'd better get back quick like. There are some dark clouds building."

The drive back to town was silent until they reached the spot where the police tape marked the murder site. "Have you heard anymore about this?" asked Cat.

"Well, rumor has it that Mr. Brockhurst might be involved."

Cat gulped when he saw the yellow tape flap in the breeze. What could have happened to that poor man? How did he die? Was Mr. Brockhurst a killer? Gilda's dad could be mean, especially when he'd been drinking. Cat was afraid of him and felt sorry for Gilda. Cat leaned back into his seat. He remembered the worry in Gilda's voice. He would talk to her tomorrow at school.

"You boys will be getting off for summer pretty soon, heh?"

"Yeah, I can't wait," said Frenchie.

"You'll have to come out to the cabin and visit. Have some hot dog roasts, do some fishing." He looked over at Frenchie hugging the far seat. "You can fish from the dock, you know. You don't have to go out in a boat to catch fish," suggested Gus.

Frenchie shrugged. "Yeah, I suppose." But it wasn't fish he was worried about catching. It was more about something catching him.

Chapter 7

The low sun peeked through some dark clouds. Soon it would disappear completely. Sparkly dew diamonds decorated the green grass of Cedarville Elementary School. A single car idled in the front parking lot. The passenger door opened and Gilda climbed out. She reached back inside for her backpack.

"I could have ridden my bike," she said looking at her mom's red eyes. Her mom was always crying these days. She was seldom happy. Why couldn't she be happy for a change? It was her father's fault. Why did he do these things that made her mom upset? Gilda couldn't believe that he was being held on suspicion of murder.

"I know you could have, dear. But I want to talk with your teacher after school anyways. After that I thought maybe we could go out for dinner. Just the two of us."

Gilda nodded. "Sure, mom. Just the two of us." Lately when her father was around, they'd had a lot of fun. She should have known it was too good to be true, that it wouldn't last.

Mrs. Brockhurst stretched over and kissed Gilda on the cheek. "I'll be by at last bell. Have a good day, honey."

Gilda closed the door and watched her mom drive away.

***

Frenchie pumped a fist into the air. He stood, leaning on his bike at the end of the driveway where it turned onto Cedar Drive.

Cat braked and stopped when the front tire of his bike bumped Frenchie's leg.

"Beat you," cheered Frenchie. He was happy to have, for the first time ever, got to their meeting place first.

Cat always had to wait for Frenchie to show up. And Frenchie always had excuses; my mom made me make my bed, my mom made me wash the dishes, my mom made me clean my room. Or Cat's favorite; my mom made me write a letter to my sick great aunt in Bolivia. But Cat knew these excuses were like "When Pigs Could Fly." Cat nodded. "So you weren't allowed to watch cartoons today, huh?"

Frenchie's mouth dropped. Busted.

As they coasted to a stop at the bike stand, a blue Dodge truck pulled into the parking lot. It was Mr. Simms, their teacher. Graying hair and moustache faded into the background when that big smile cracked the surface. If you asked the kids they would say Mr. Simms was always smiling. He would no sooner break up a schoolyard fight, than his smile would calm the combatants into friendly resolution of their problem.

"Good morning, boys."

"Good morning, Mr. S." They referred to Mr. Simms as Mr. S when conversing privately but opted for his official title when in public.

"Ready for your news report this morning, William?"

Cat suddenly felt a flash of panic. He was supposed to present a news story for the class today. But after the crazy weekend at the lake, he'd completely forgotten about the assignment. Cat had made quite a name for himself regarding class news reports. How could he forget? This was something he lived for.

"Yes sir," Cat mumbled.

Mr. Simms looked at his watch, "See you in twenty minutes." As Mr. Simms disappeared into the school, the boys walked over to the swings.

"Geez, Frenchie. I forgot all about my news report."

"Well why don't you tell about that guy's murder. You could tell stuff that Gus told us. Like the body hanging in a tree. Now that's one heck of a story."

"Yeah, but that stuff is not official."

"Who cares? It's terrific; the class would eat it up! If the Vancouver Province had this stuff it would be front page."

As they rounded the corner of the building, there was Gilda on the swing. Cat stopped and pulled on Frenchie's shirt to stop. "There's who cares. Her dad is in trouble here, Frenchie."

"Oh, yeah, I forgot about that."

As they sauntered over, Gilda stopped swinging and quickly rubbed at her eyes.

"Hi," said Cat. He noticed the sadness. She was the "old Gilda". The one who walked on eggshells in public, fearing public scrutiny. Wishing she could be a shadow unnoticed by humanity. Unfortunately, Cat's intuition was not on Frenchie's radar.

"Hey is your dad still in jail?" Frenchie blurted out.

Cat reached back and punched Frenchie hard on the shoulder.

"Ouch! What did you do that for?"

Suddenly Gilda's face flushed and a wild look flashed in her eyes. Like a person metamorphosing into a Werewolf.

"He didn't do anything," she growled. Then she stormed off towards the building.

***

"Okay. News report time. Cat? You have something for us today?" asked Mr. Simms.

Cat stood up. Now what? He looked over at Frenchie. Frenchie just shrugged. No help there. He looked over at Gilda. She had her head buried in her arms on her desk, refusing eye contact with anyone.

"Uh..." Cat could feel everyone's eyes on him. "No, Mr. Simms. Sorry I forgot about the assignment." He sat down.

"Mr. star reporter," joked Mr. Simms. "You don't have a juicy story for us today?" Mr. Simms sensed a problem, but he didn't push it. Instead he smiled and said, "Well I'll give you a second chance next week. Think that would work for you, William." Mr. Simms was all about second chances, if he felt the student deserved them. But there were never any third chances. After two you lost marks.

"Yes, thanks, Mr. Simms." Cat breathed a sigh of relief. Frenchie breathed a sigh of relief. Gilda lifted her head. There was no relief on her face, just gloom.

Unfortunately, this wasn't going to go away. Gilda's life was never that easy. Steven Brown had his hand raised. Short and skinny, Steven Brown used whatever means necessary to be "seen". He was willing to use his loud voice and stretch the truth to become the center of attention. So when Mr. Simms saw Steven waving his hand, he checked to see if there were any other student's hands up. "Anybody else have some news," he asked, almost in a pleading voice. But Mr. Simms was fair and willing to take risks to show he cared about all of his students. Reluctantly, he called on Steven.

Steven made his way to the front of the class. "There was a man killed up near Cultus Lake." As he held up the newspaper clipping, Gilda cringed back down. If she could have, she would have crawled into her desk.

The room was so quiet you could have heard a pin drop. Steven grinned. Something he shouldn't do. Missing a tooth from mouthing off at a grade four student who may have been younger but was taller and packed a solid punch, the grin made him look dopey. Not that he had many smarts to begin with. Whether he was socially stupid or just mean, no one in that room, including Mr. Simms, knew. But no one else in the room would have been so mean as to say, "They are holding a suspect. And my dad says Mr. Brockhurst has been arrested."

Before Mr. Simms or anyone else could react, Gilda dashed out of the room.

Chapter 8

Gilda spent the rest of the morning at the office. Mrs. Cook, the principal, talked to her about the incident, calming her down and reassuring Gilda of her value to the class and school. That one person saying cruel things could not diminish Gilda in the eyes of her friends. But Gilda was not ready to go back to class, so she relaxed in an alcove that had a desk and chair and, more importantly, was hidden from any visitors. Mr. Simms sent some work for her to do.

When the lunch bell rang, Cat and Frenchie showed up.

"And what can I do for you gentlemen?" asked Mrs. Cook.

"We have Gilda's lunch."

The boys convinced Mrs. Cook to let them eat outside in their favorite spot, as long as they cleaned up and didn't leave any litter.

Gilda sat at the nearby picnic table while the boys chose to eat while swinging.

"We should tape Steven's mouth shut," said Cat swallowing a bite of sandwich.

"No, crazy glue," suggested Frenchie.

"Yeah, he is crazy," said Gilda. Frenchie laughed and Gilda broke out her famous smile. Cat nodded, lost in that smile. He would do anything for that smile, he thought.

After lunch Gilda went back to the classroom, Cat and Frenchie close by her side. First of all Steven apologized. Mr. Simms had convinced Steven it was in his best interest. The rest of the class agreed. Most of them had come to like Gilda after the incident of the lost pets. Only Steven and a couple of others would take opportunities to bully if given a chance.

Mr. Simms thought his day could not get any more complicated. But as fate would have it, a new student appeared at his door. The boy had a transfer and quite a large file from a school in Vancouver. From experience, Mr. Simms expected a large file to mean problems. Academic or behavioral or both. But he always liked to give the new student a chance to start fresh. Give them a clean slate and the tools to provide them success.

"Class this is Robert George. He will be joining us for this last month, so make sure you show him around and make him welcome."

Cat observed the boy. He looked like he should be in grade eight. The dark skinned youth was only inches shorter than Mr. Simms. His close cropped hair reminded Cat of the "crew cut" he had in grade one. Robert's brown face showed no emotion, his lips pursed in determination. Like he was forcing himself to withstand the inspecting eyes of twenty-nine strangers.

"Robert you can take that empty desk," said Mr. Simms pointing to the back of the room.

Robert moved smoothly, for someone so big. As he sat in the chair, his knees brushed the underside of the desk. He looked like an adult stuffed into a child's place.

As Mr. Simms started teaching, the class soon lost interest in the new boy. Much to Robert's relief. They were working on creative writing; practicing all the skills they had learned up until now. The topic today was fairy tales. Mr. Simms discussed with them the typical roles of the characters, how they were often exaggerated and an element of evil was the focus to overcome.

At the mention of evil, many of the class mumbled the word "evil". And it was like Cat could read Frenchie's mind and vice versa. They both immediately thought of the Beaton family. Gilda normally would have had the same thought, but at the moment the only evil on her mind was what her dad was supposedly involved in.

"Your assignment," said Mr. Simms, is to choose a well known fairy tale and change it to make it your own story. You may work in groups, but each of you will be responsible for writing a copy. Any questions?"

Steven Brown put up his hand.

Mr. Simms looked over at Steven. "Besides Steven?" Steven slowly sucked his arm back down.

"William, may Robert work with your group?"

Cat, who was headed over to Frenchie's desk, stopped in his tracks. "Uh...yeah...sure."

Cat changed direction and Frenchie followed him over to Robert. "Hi, I'm Cat."

Robert sitting in his chair was nearly face to face with Cat. "Okay...uh...Cat?" He thought that a strange name until Cat explained. Frenchie did likewise.

"And so because I speak French, they call me Frenchie."

"Well, in that case you may call me "Halkomelem.""

Puzzled, they looked at Robert whose face remained stoic. He offered no other information and they could not tell if he was serious or joking. When it looked as if no other information was forthcoming, Frenchie had to ask, "Halko...what?"

In his monotone voice, Robert continued, "My family are Sto:lo. That means river people. The language they speak is Halkomelem."

"Halko...,"Cat tried.

"...melem," finished Robert.

Just then Gilda walked over and introduced herself as Gilda. "That's it, just Gilda. Although I've been called a lot of bad nicknames in my time. So I'll stick with plain old Gilda, thank you very much."

"Okay. Well let's choose a fairy tale to write about," said Cat.

"How about Hansel and Gretel?" said Gilda. "I always liked that one."

"You mean where those two kids get lost and meet up with this old lady who offers them treats to come visit her?" asked Frenchie.

"Yeah that's the one Einstein," teased Cat. Gilda chuckled.

"Ou'xia," said Robert. Again there was puzzled silence.

"Uh...what?" said Cat.

"Ou'xia, the cannibal woman. The Sto:lo tell the story of an old short, stout woman who would call all the children "grandchildren" She would tell them to close their eyes to get something good to eat. Then she'd pitch their eyes closed, throw them in her basket and take them home to eat."

"Wow," said Gilda. "That must have been one big basket. But that story is quite similar to Hansel and Gretel, isn't it?"

"Yeah," said Frenchie. "Only I never thought of the old woman as a cannibal."

"Hey, that's great Robert. We can make our own fairy tale using your...uh...Halk...o...mel...em story."

And I've got the perfect nickname for you," said Frenchie looking across at Robert. "The Halk." They all laughed. All except Robert, who stood up.

"No," said Robert. The other three suddenly were very quiet. They almost held their breath wondering if they'd made Robert mad.

A slow smile blossomed into a full blown grin as Robert said," The Incredible Halk."

As their laughter spilled out, Mr. Simms had to tell them to keep it down.

Chapter 9

Surrounded by her friends, Gilda had a fun afternoon and forgot her troubles. But when she spotted her mom at the classroom door, everything resurfaced. Sitting in her desk, she watched the class erupt like a volcano when the bell went. Sliding chairs noisily plunked on desktops, children laughed and talked while shoving homework into backpacks. As her mom stepped towards the teacher's desk, Gilda saw Frenchie and Cat wave at her. She wished she could leave with them. Why couldn't she have a normal life like them? She waved back and forced a smile. In minutes silence reigned. Her mom motioned for her to join them.

The meeting went well, Mr. Simms understood the stress the Brockhursts were under. He offered to help in any way he could. He would allow for the strain on Gilda in assigning marks for her. He would give her extra help if she needed it, after school or at lunch. He welcomed them both to see him if they needed to talk.

Those morning cotton ball clouds had thickened and darkened, like marshmallows being slowly roasted over a campfire. A light rain sprinkled her face as she climbed into the car's passenger side.

"So dad has to stay in jail?"

"Yes, dear. He said to say hi and that he loves you very much."

"When will he come home?"

"The trial is in two weeks. We don't have any money for his bail, so he'll have to stay there until after the trial."

Gilda gulped, swallowing the fear of her next question like it was some foul medicine. But she had to ask. "Is he guilty, mom?"

Her mom hesitated, not expecting this. "No. No, of course not, honey. Your father couldn't kill anyone. Sure, he gets angry sometimes, when he's been..." She couldn't say the shameful word. "Why, he couldn't even kill a chicken. Remember those chickens we had that were due to be slaughtered?"

Gilda smiled thinking back to that day. Her mom and dad had explained to her what had to be done. It might seem cruel but there came a time when all things must die, some in order to feed others. They had raised the chickens for food. And today was the day they would need to be slaughtered. She stayed in her bedroom. She tried reading a book, but kept thinking of what was happening in the barn. The minutes passed slowly. Finally she couldn't stand the suspense. She needed to see what happened. She rushed out of the house, despite her mother's cry to wait inside. When she got to the barn, the doors were wide open and there were chickens wandering all over. She slowly stepped around them and peeked inside. There was her dad, sitting on the "beheading" stump, his shoulders slumped his head resting on top of the axe handle. When she laughed, his head popped up. Just then a chicken swooped and landed on his shoulder. His face was dead serious as he said, "What are you looking at?"

"A chicken?" said Gilda, pointing at him.

Her dad started laughing and Gilda too. They laughed so hard tears came.

"Where do you want to go for dinner," asked her mom, breaking her daydream.

"Can we just go home, mom. I need to see Chester."

"Sure," said Mrs. Brockhurst a little surprised. "Sure, how 'bout I whip up some pancakes for supper. And I've got some fresh strawberries and whipped cream."

As they pulled into the driveway, Chester barked and bounced beside the car. Mrs. Brockhurst was always worried she'd run him over, but he seemed to know just when to move away. Gilda hugged him as he licked her face.

After putting her school stuff away in her bedroom, she wandered out to play with Chester. He flipped an old tennis ball at her feet. Picking up the saliva coated ball she threw it as far as she could. It sailed into the open barn door. Chester eagerly bounded after it. But when he didn't reappear right away Gilda followed him.

The cool, damp air inside had that farm smell. A mixture of wet hay, manure and cow smell. Chester was over by the ladder leading to the loft, his front feet on the third or fourth rung like he wanted to climb up. He was moaning; that dog cry he used when he wanted something.

"What's up, Chester? Your ball is over here." She picked it up and threw it back outside. But Chester remained straddling the ladder.

Bessie and Tillie mooed their welcome. Gilda shuffled into their stall. She stroked their heads as their long tails swept flies from their backs. "You guys need more hay?"

Chester jumped down and sat while Gilda climbed the first rung. But as she reached the top, he began barking and running in circles.

Gilda looked down. "Okay, okay. I'm just getting some hay. I'll be right back." It was gloomy in the loft. Thin streamers of light filtered through cracks in the old siding. Hay stack towers, six bales high, nearly completely filled the floor. Except for the nearest stack which was spread out like it had fallen. Bales were strewn about. When her eyes grew accustomed to the dark, she stepped over and grabbed the wires holding the first bale. Suddenly something covered her face. She couldn't see. And the scream in her throat came out as a muffled groan.

***

Frenchie met Cat at the bike stand. "What do you think Gilda's mom wants?"

Cat dialed the numbers on the combination lock and pulled it open. "Probably just to tell Mr. Simms stuff about Mr. Brockhurst. I don't know?"

Frenchie puffed out a breath. "Cat, do you think he did it? Killed that guy?"

Cat shrugged. "I know Gilda doesn't think so. And that's good enough for me."

Robert George appeared, pushing his bike. The bike was kid size, which made Robert look ridiculous next to it. "Ride home with you guys?"

Cat smiled at him. "You ride that thing?"

Robert nodded. "Yeah. I need a new bike, but we don't have any money. Beats walking."

"Where do you live?" asked Frenchie.

"In an old farm house just across the tracks."

Cat's eyes widened. "Does it have an old silo with a faded white dome and mossy gray sides?"

"Yeah. Do you know the place?"

Cat and Frenchie nodded at the same time. "Yeah. We know it."

Although Robert looked like one of those clowns at the circus who ride tiny bikes, he somehow managed to stay balanced and his strong legs pushed the pedals a mile a minute. Cat and Frenchie had a hard time trying to keep up. They didn't stop until they reached the driveway leading to the Beaton's farm. What used to be the Beaton's place. Now there was a mini van parked where old man Beaton's truck used to be.

Frenchie gulped as he looked towards the barn. Like a ghost it still scared him.

Chapter 10

Gilda's heart raced. She squirmed but felt strong arms holding her. "Mom!" she shouted in her mind. She could hear Chester barking and then a voice calmed her fears.

"Shh, it's okay Gilda." The hand left her eyes and she looked into her father's face.

"Wha...what are you doing here?"

"Well I came to visit."

"But aren't you supposed to be in ..." Gilda didn't want to say it.

"In jail. Yeah well they are saying I did something I didn't do. It's not right. So I gotta find the answer. Will you help me, Gilda?"

Gilda rubbed her eye. She took a deep breath, trying to figure things out. Too much was happening all at once. Her dad was supposed to be in jail. But he was asking her for help. She couldn't remember her dad ever asking her for help. Did her mom know?

As if he could read her mind, he said, "Gilda don't tell mom, okay?"

"What are you going to do, dad?"

"I'm going to hide out for a while and see if I can figure this thing out. Up on the mountain. But I need a few things. Could you get some stuff for me without mom finding out?"

Gilda closed her eyes and tried to think. Her dad was an escaped prisoner. But if he was innocent, then he shouldn't even be in jail. How could he survive living up on Spirit Mountain?

"Gilda, please I need your help."

Gilda opened her eyes. Sure her dad had been mean to her when he'd been drinking. But he'd also been good to her at other times. And he was her only dad. "Okay. What do you need?"

First this. He gave her a hug.

***

Robert found the doors locked. "I guess mom is still at work. She just got a job at the Public Library.

"Well don't you have a key?" asked Cat.

"No. We just moved here last weekend. Mom hasn't had time to make extra keys, yet."

"Maybe we should go," said Frenchie, quietly, more to himself than the other two.

"I know. Let's go out to the barn," said Robert. "I haven't had time to check it out. It looks like a cool hideout."

Cat said, "I need to tell you something, Robert." As Cat filled in Robert about their adventures in that barn, Frenchie walked towards the bushes at the side of the house.

"I gotta go, guys. And I don't mean away," mumbled Frenchie. Cat and Robert watched unconcerned.

Once out of sight, Frenchie was about to unzip, when a scratchy high pitched voice stopped him. Whipping his head around Frenchie saw a little, old lady carrying a basket slowly stepping towards him. A bright woven shawl covered her tiny head and shoulders.

Frenchie's eyes opened wide and he felt his knees shake. And he was dangerously close to peeing himself.

"My grandson, would you like a treat? Come and see what I have in my basket."

Frenchie turned and ran.

***

After supper, Gilda told her mom she needed to go and feed Chester. She planned to bring her dad the stuff he had asked for.

"Okay. I'll go with you. I could use some fresh air," her mom answered.

"Uh, actually, mom the barn gets kinda stinky. I need to shovel a bit of...you know."

"Come on,' chuckled Mrs. Brockhurst. "I'm used to that smell."

"I was going to shovel out the stink, mom. Why don't you wait until that's done?"

"Nonsense, Gilda. I'll help you. I've shoveled more ...you know, then you've seen in your whole life." She slipped into a jacket.

Gilda was running out of ideas. Finally she resorted to, "I'd like to be alone, mom. I've got some thinking to do."

Her mom's smile faded. "I know this has been hard on you, Gilda. But it will work out." She wrapped her arms around Gilda. "Okay. Go talk to Chester for awhile."

Gilda was home free. For a second.

"What's that stuff?" Her mom pointed to the backpack and blankets under the bench.

"Uh...just some stuff, mom."

"But what do you need blankets for?"

"Uh... I was just ...uh..."

Mrs. Brockhurst was reaching down when the phone rang. "I wonder who that could be?" As soon as her mom went to answer, Gilda picked up the stuff.

"Hello?" answered Mrs. Brockhurst. "Oh hello, Sergeant MacFarlane."

***

Cat and Robert had just opened the barn's huge front door, when they heard the scream. It was a cross between a wolf howl and a sick rooster. When Cat saw Frenchie running towards them, he stifled a laugh. Frenchie had proven he could move quickly on several occasions. But the windmilling arms and chest thrust forward like an orangutan, reminded him of an out-of-water swimmer, and always made him laugh. Not to mention Frenchie's crooked glasses somehow hanging onto his bobbing face.

"Ou'xia!" yelled Frenchie.

Cat couldn't make out what Frenchie was trying to say. But Robert did. "Ou'xia?" he whispered.

"Run," panted Frenchie as he ran past them into the barn.

"What's with him?" asked Cat.

Just then the old lady appeared around the side of the house. "Grandchildren, so good to see you," she said approaching them. "Would you like something good to eat?" She reached inside her basket. "Close your eyes and open your mouth."

Cat's mouth dropped, but not because he was hungry. Robert saw his face and started laughing.

"What's so funny my grandchild?" The wrinkles on her face stretched up when she smiled, so that she appeared to have dozens of smiles.

"Grandma, this is my friend, William Katt."

"Pleased to meet you, young man." She shook Cat's hand. Cat nodded. Frenchie poked his head out the barn door.

"Pleased to meet you too, young man. I didn't know I looked so frightening."

Chapter 11

Gilda moved as quickly as she could carrying the blankets and backpack. Dark clouds billowed as a cool wind signaled rain. Chester met her at the bottom of the stairs, wagging his tail furiously. As she hustled towards the barn, Chester thought she was playing a game and leaped around her. His interference slowed her. "Chester, get out of the way." When she reached the barn door a large raindrop splashed her nose. She was about to put the stuff down, when the door partially slid open, a hand grabbed her and pulled her inside.

Closing the door behind them her dad took the blankets from her. "Thanks Gilda. These'll do just fine." He wrapped them inside an orange tarp.

"Dad, Sergeant MacFarlane is on the phone talking to mom."

He looked at her concerned face. "Don't worry, Gilda. It'll work out." He took the backpack from her. He used some baling string to tie the tarp on. He adjusted the straps as far as they would go, and squeezed the pack onto his back. "Guess I'm too big for school." He let out a nervous laugh.

Gilda managed a smile. "Actually it used to be Frenchie's."

"Well it'll do." He stepped forward and pulled Gilda to his chest. "I love you, honey."

"I love you too, dad." Her chest felt tight and her eyes watered.

He nodded and let her go. Carefully opening the door, rain whipped into his face. He pulled a hood over his head and cinched it tight. He looked over his shoulder and gave Gilda a wink, then pressed out into the storm.

Gilda watched her dad until he was out of sight. She knelt beside Chester who was sitting looking out into the rain. He offered a paw. She gave him a 'pawshake', then a hug. They wandered over to Bessie and Tillie, feeding them some hay.

"Gilda is your father here?"

Her mom's voice startled her. Mrs. Brockhurst stood just inside the door, water dripping from saturated hair.

Gilda stood. "No. He's...uh...not here."

"Gilda I just talked to Sergeant MacFarlane, and he said your father escaped from jail."

"He did?" Gilda tried to sound surprised.

"Yes. And then I wondered why you needed blankets." She moved past Gilda, checking the corners of the barn. She was about to climb the ladder to the loft, when Gilda stopped her.

"He's not there, mom. He just left."

Mrs. Brockhurst stepped down and walked back to Gilda. Placing her hands on Gilda's shoulders, she asked, "Where's he going?"

"Mom, he just wants to figure things out."

"But how can he figure things out? He's already in trouble. Why can't he ever do things right?" Mrs. Brockhurst started crying.

Gilda hugged her mom while Chester moaned nearby. They huddled inside the barn until the damp chill forced them to dash inside the house.

***

When the first blast of thunder hit, Robert, Cat and Frenchie were safely inside the house. Robert's grandmother had a key and she'd invited them all inside for a snack.

"Grandmother always wants to feed us." said Robert sitting at the kitchen table.

She reached out a withered hand and rumpled his hair. "You are a big boy who needs his nourishment."

"The Incredible Halk," joked Cat.

Robert belted out a laugh. Seeing the puzzled look on his grandmother's face, he explained the nickname.

She said, "Yes, our people the Sto:lo speak the Halkomelem language." As she related some more information about Robert's kin, Frenchie was caught in a time warp remembering the last time he was in that kitchen. He slowly turned an eye towards the refrigerator. He saw Sergeant MacFarlane opening the door, and bloody meat dripping inside. The bear organs wrapped in cellophane. His mother screaming. So when Grandmother George opened the door to get them some milk, he stood and let out a cry, "No!"

The room went silent. Grandma held the door open while everyone looked at Frenchie. "You really don't have to drink any if you don't want, "she said in a puzzled tone. She lifted out the jug of milk and carried it to the table. She poured some for Cat who held his glass out. "Don't worry about, Frenchie, Grandma George. He gets these weird fits sometimes." Chuckling he dipped his large peanut butter cookie into the milk and took a big bite.

"Did you get a new fridge?" asked Frenchie.

"Oh, yeah," said Robert. "Grandma said the old one was haunted."

"Haunted?" asked Cat.

"Oh, yes. There were bad sprits coming from that one," said Grandma George. "Bad spirits that would poison the food."

"Grandma had us haul the old one to the dump."

See, "said Frenchie, punching Cat on the shoulder. "Anything those Beatons touched was poisoned."

"I better phone home, "announced Cat after finishing off his cookies and milk.

"Our phone doesn't work yet," said Robert. "Sorry."

"Too bad I don't have my cell phone yet," said Frenchie.

"Well, I guess we better start riding."

"Nonsense. I will give you a ride, "said Grandma George."

So they squeezed their bikes into the back of the van and watched the storm from the dry safety of the soft vinyl backseat. Well what they thought was safety.

"You boys okay back there?" asked Grandma, turning around while driving.

"Grandma, move over! You're in the middle of the road," said Robert from the passenger seat.

"Not to worry Robert. There's plenty of room."

"You're supposed to leave the other half of the road for cars going the other way." Robert turned to talk to Cat and Frenchie. "Grandma thinks she can use the whole road when there's no traffic. Like she owns it." Suddenly he was thrown against the door as the van swerved.

"Did you see that squirrel?" Grandma looked in her rearview mirror, then not seeing anything turned to look out the side window. The van churned up gravel from the shoulder. Seeing the squirrel safely on the other side, she inched back into her lane.

Robert had his eyes covered. "This is where you might want to cover your eyes and wait for something good to eat."

"Ha, ha, ha. You boys are in good hands with your old Grandma."

Frenchie was glad he couldn't see out the front. He reached for the handgrip above the window. He saw a man walking along the opposite shoulder. As the van passed him, Frenchie saw his face.

"Sacre bleu." He poked Cat who just caught a peek at the man's face before the van went over the hill.

"Mr. Brockhurst?" whispered Cat.

Frenchie nodded. "I thought he was in jail."

Chapter 12

As the rain flew horizontally in his face, Mr. Brockhurst took long strides along the railway tracks. He was heading towards Spirit Mountain. Water had already seeped through his hood and he felt the first trickle down his neck. Fortunately the temperature was a pleasant fifteen degrees Celsius. But it would drop significantly by nightfall, so he would need to find some kind of shelter.

Halfway across the railway trestle, he looked down at the Thuwelman River rushing beneath him. It was running high and with this heavy rainfall would continue to rise. Thanks to dikes built along the river, it had been years since his low farmland had been flooded. Still, if they had lots of these rainy days, it was a possibility. He swallowed a lump of guilt. His family was on their own. He'd screwed up again. How was he going to get out of this one? He gazed down at the swirling muddy water.

***

Cat rode his bike on the edge of the road trying to avoid puddles. Usually he wouldn't care. But he had a whole day yet ahead of him. His mom had been thankful to Mrs. George for driving him home. She'd tried phoning home but the storm had knocked out the power and the phone lines. She was worried about him being home alone without any electricity. She'd phoned Mrs. Boudreau on her cell and found out the boys were at Robert George's, a new boy. When Frenchie arrived home with Cat, Mrs. Boudreau phoned Mrs. Katt back to let her know the boys were safe.

The power had been off when Cat went to bed and he'd hoped it would be off in the morning so there would be no school. No such luck.

As Cat pulled his bike to a stop at the end of Evergreen Street, he looked up towards the tracks. What had Gilda's father been doing? Wasn't he supposed to be in jail? He'd wanted to phone Gilda to ask, but of course he couldn't.

He mounted his bike and headed towards Frenchie's. He hadn't ridden far when he saw someone standing with a bike at the end of Frenchie's driveway. It was Gilda. What was she doing here?

He picked up speed to meet her. Skidding to a stop, he greeted her. "Hey, Gilda. I wanted to phone you last night but that storm knocked out the power lines."

She gave a quick nod, then the floodgates opened. "Cat, my dad escaped from jail and my mom's worried he's going to get hurt, I gave him some stuff, but I wonder if he made it through the storm okay, and if he will find a place to stay and what will the police do to him if they catch him?" She swallowed a sob.

"Uh...yeah. We saw him yesterday during the storm. He was walking along the railway tracks."

Gilda took a deep breath. "Cat, he's in big trouble."

Cat gulped.

"But I know that he's innocent," Gilda affirmed.

"Maybe we can help?"

"How?"

"Uh...well I don't know. But I think this is a "Y" file. There's more to this case than what the police know. Something happened at Cultus Lake. Frenchie says he saw something in the water, too."

Gilda wiped her tears.

Cat squinted up the road he had just pedaled down. Another biker was coming. Was that who he thought?

"Hey that looks like Robert," said Gilda.

"He really needs a bigger bike," laughed Cat.

When Robert reached them, he braked and pulled a wheelie. This resulted in him standing, holding the bike in front of him. "Let's see you do that."

"I'd need to grow another couple feet taller, first," chided Cat.

"Hi guys. Hey, I brought my glove and ball. Do you like baseball, Cat?"

Cat grinned. "Do bears go number two in the woods?"

"Hey what about me?" asked Gilda.

"Do you like baseball?"

"Does Frenchie ride like a girl?" said Gilda spotting Frenchie weaving his twelve speed down the driveway. They all laughed.

"Ce qui se passe? What's up?" asked Frenchie, awkwardly dismounting his bike.

"Hey Ke-mo-sah-bee, "said Robert.

They all looked at Robert like he had sworn or something. He kept coming up with these things. Things that surprised them. How did he know this stuff?

"What?" Robert puzzled over their silence. "What? It's from an old TV show my grandma watches. She likes Tonto, the Indian. He was Potawatomi. He saved the Lone Ranger and if it wasn't for him there would be no show."

Frenchie poked around in his pack. "Hey that reminds me. Look what I got!"

"You got your cell phone?" said Cat. "But I thought you had to wait until Friday."

"Yeah, but with that storm, and us not able to phone because the lines were down, mom gave it to me early."

"Cool," said Robert.

"Smile, Incredible Halk," said Frenchie holding the phone up.

"You can take pictures with yours?" asked Gilda.

75

"Yep," said Frenchie shooting her picture before she could cover her face.

"Let's see," said Cat. Frenchie backed away from Cat's reaching hand and snapped his picture. Then he held out the camera for all to see.

"Just don't get caught with that at school." said Gilda. Cedarville Elementary did not allow kids to have cell phones.

"Yeah, yeah. My mom told me to make sure it was turned off and keep it in my backpack. But because of that storm, she is going to the next PTA meeting to ask about changing the cell phone policy. Kids need them for safety."

"All right, Mrs. Boudreau," cheered Cat. "Maybe then my mom would get me one, too."

Just then the school bell rang.

"Sacre bleu," snorted Frenchie. "We're going to be late."

The foursome pedaled like they were in a race. They didn't have time to notice the clouds building and darkening.

Chapter 13

Mr. Brockhurst went from sound asleep, to wide awake in seconds. Loud engine noise and metal wheels squealing scared him awake. He felt like there was a train on top of him, which there was. He'd found shelter last night under the train bridge. He'd managed to put on dry clothes and nestling in the blankets and tarp, he'd kept warm. It had rained most of the night.

When the train had departed, he gingerly crawled out of the covers. After bundling them all up and fastening them to his pack, he shook out his raincoat. It was too wet to put on, so he draped it over his pack. He put the pack on and carefully climbed out from under the bridge.

Bright sunshine greeted him. Its warmth massaged his face. But he noticed dark clouds forming like enormous dirty soap bubbles. More rain was coming. He watched the river exerting its power. It had risen since yesterday and was threatening to overspill its banks.

Walking comfortably along the trail at the foot of Spirit Mountain, he reached the "murder site" in less than an hour. He knew this was the site, because yellow police tape hung in tatters from the bushes. Mr. Brockhurst scanned the area. So this was the place.

***

Robert, Frenchie, Cat and Gilda worked on their fairy tale writing assignment. They had decided to script a play for their version of Hansel and Gretel. Gilda had yet to offer any ideas. In fact she had hadn't said more than hi all morning. She kept wondering about her dad.

At recess they met at their usual spot. Gilda sat on a swing, while the boys took turns snapping pictures using Frenchie's cell phone.

Robert did his "Incredible Halk" pose, biceps pumped up in the air. Cat hung upside down from the top of the swings. Frenchie put his glasses, jacket and hat on backwards so Cat could take his picture from the back. "The hairy face nerd," said Robert.

"Hey Gilda, smile," said Cat holding the phone in front of her face. She ducked her head. He poked the phone under her hair. She turned to the left. He swung the phone to the left. She turned to the right. He swung the phone to the right.

"Cut it out," she barked. But there was a big smile on her face. Cat took the shot. He sat on the swing next to her as Robert and Frenchie walked over.

"I'm sorry, you guys. I can't stop thinking about my dad."

"Well I say we go find him," said Cat.

"Yeah," said Robert. "We could bring him some food."

"But we don't have a clue where he is," said Frenchie.

"Actually we do have a clue. He was walking on the tracks towards Spirit Mountain. I'm thinking he was headed towards Cultus Lake. Maybe to try to find an empty cabin," said Cat.

"The eeeevil spirit lake," moaned Robert, trying to sound scary.

"What?" asked Frenchie.

"Oh yeah. The name Cultus is a Halkomelem word meaning bad. My grandma told me the Sto:lo believed Cultus Lake was the home of slalakums or evil spirits."

Cat gulped and his eyes widened. Frenchie's eyes swelled like flowers opening in the sun. "Wha...wha...what?" he stuttered.

"Hey, what's with you guys. It's just a legend."

"Frenchie saw something in the water when we were fishing the other day," said Cat. Frenchie nodded emphatically.

"Yeah?" replied Robert.

"And my dad says Fred Smith saw something in the lake the day he was killed," said Gilda.

Robert shrugged. "That's all I know. But my grandpa has all these stories. He's the one we should talk to."

"Where does he live?" asked Cat.

"At Cultus Lake, of course. He has a cabin right on the beach. He's lived there for many years. He says he was the first one there. Well after the Slalakum that is."

"I bet Gus knows him," said Cat.

"Well why don't we go and visit him after school," replied Robert.

"Ah...that's kinda far to ride," said Frenchie.

"No, I'm sure my grandma would drive us," offered Robert.

Frenchie and Cat clenched their teeth and shook, pretending to be scared. "It might be safer to swim across," joked Cat. But part of him was serious. Robert's grandma was a terrible driver.

"Oh come on you guys. She's never been in an accident. Well except for wiping out a fence."

They all looked at him.

"Well it was either hit the cow or hit the fence. It's a long story."

***

Gazing up into the cedar trees, Mr. Brockhurst couldn't decide which was the tree where they'd found Fred. He was about to leave when he saw a scrap of yellow tape in the bark of one. He walked around the huge cedar and found more yellow flagging tape behind it. This must be the one, he thought, gazing up the tremendously huge tree. The first branch was about ten feet up. He jumped but was unable to touch it. Well how was I ever supposed to have climbed this tree, let alone carried Fred's body up? It didn't make sense. The police should be able to figure that out. But Fred had been shot. And with his rifle. That was why he was the number one suspect. But the police had never found his rifle. It must have fallen into the lake. Mr. Brockhurst gazed up at that first branch. Who did this? What the heck happened out there on the lake? He wished he could remember something to help. Fred was fishing and spitting his tobacco juice in the water, when he said he saw something. Then he went nuts. What had he seen?

A large raindrop hit Mr. Brockhurst's face. He returned to the trail leading up the mountain. Once again the clouds ruptured spilling their liquid cargo. After half an hour of slogging along the muddy trail, Mr. Brockhurst came to a clearing. At the far end was a cabin. He knew this place.

It was the hunters' cabin that the Beatons had made famous with their bear poaching. Gilda had told him most of that story, except how she managed to escape them. That part of the story never seemed to make sense. But he'd never pursued it. Happy just that she was safe.

He forced open the crooked front door and closed it. The cabin was cold. And smelled like his hunting clothes after a couple of week's sweat. He was beginning to smell like that already. Removing his wet clothes he draped them over the twine clothesline running across the ceiling over the woodstove. He was tempted to light it, but the smoke would draw attention. He would have to dry out as best as possible without it. And he would not be able to stay long, as the police were sure to check this place out. And they would have the dogs. Geez, what was he going to do when the dogs were sent? He better not stay too long. He needed to keep moving.

Chapter 14

The school day couldn't go by fast enough. Cat watched the minute hand close in on the twelve, so when the 3:00 bell rang he was ready to beat the rush. Frenchie, Gilda and Robert joined him at the bike rack. The rain had stopped but huge puddles like mini lakes dotted the school grounds.

They rode to Frenchie's house first. Reluctantly, Frenchie's mom gave him permission to go to Robert's grandparents' place on Cultus Lake, providing he was home before dark. And he kept his cell phone handy.

Cat used Frenchie's phone to call the hospital where Mrs. Katt worked. She was busy so he left a message with the receptionist.

The next stop was Gilda's. Chester bounded out to greet them, taking time to sniff their legs and lick petting hands. He was wary of Robert, as he'd not met him before, but instantly welcomed him as a friend.

He hung particularly close to Frenchie. "You smell Spud and Shep, heh boy?"

"Oh, that's what that smell is," joked Cat.

"Ha, ha, very funny."

Gilda, who had gone inside, came back out with a disappointed look. "My mom's not home. She left me a note saying that she should be back around six. I wonder what she' doing?"

"Probably just a milk and bread run," said Cat.

"Yeah...maybe. But I better wait here, just in case."

The boys left Gilda and rode to Robert's. Grandma's van was parked in the driveway. They expected to meet her in the house, but she wasn't to be found, so they headed outside. Frenchie watched while Cat and Robert entered the barn, still preferring to avoid that place.

"Hello?" yelled Cat.

"It's no use yelling," said Robert. "Her hearing is not so good."

They searched everywhere but the barn was empty.

"She might be out by the river," said Robert. The farmland, although mostly grassland, was bordered by the Thuwelman River to the east.

They could hear the rushing water as they got closer. "Grandma loves the river," said Robert. "She often..."

"Look," cried Cat. Grandma's still body was lying near the river, her face in the water. He raced to help. But Robert just slowly followed with a grin on his face.

Cat plunged his hands into the water and pulled her head out. Grandma's eyes popped open. "What are you doing?" she cackled. She sat up. "You scared the bejeesus out of me."

Flabbergasted, Cat stood. "Well you scared me too!"

Robert chuckled, "Grandma likes to talk to the fish."

Cat shook his head, hands on his hips. "What?"

"Yeah, she is always trying to be one with nature. So she talks to the fish. Asking them to be bountiful and give themselves for our food."

Frenchie who had caught up to them said, "My mom talks to a grocer."

"Grandma says Mother Nature is our grocer. And we should respect her."

"Mother Nature is angry," said Grandma. "See how the water lashes against the bank trying to be free."

"Yeah the water is high," replied Cat.

When they had finally loaded their bikes into the van and begun the drive to Cultus Lake, the sky had renewed its black face. Mother Nature's dark side. The boys were playing "Rock, Paper, Scissors" in the back seat, oblivious to it all. As they crossed the bridge, Grandma noticed the Thuwelman River licking the road's shoulder. She whistled softly, but kept on her way. Little did she know they wouldn't get back.

***

Mrs. Brockhurst nodded. Sergeant MacFarlane held up a blue scarf sporting a Vancouver Canuck's logo. She had given it to her husband last year at Christmas.

"Yes, that's Harold's."

"One of the dogs found it underneath the railway bridge."

Ellie Brockhurst nodded, a tear in her eye.

"Ellie, did he come to the house?"

She looked down. "I didn't see him." Which was true, she hadn't seen him, although she knew he'd been there.

"Well, we think he might be hiding out at Cultus Lake. Ellie this is not good. Him running makes him look guilty."

Ellie looked up, tears rolling down. "Harold wouldn't kill anybody."

"We've learned he and Fred were into gambling, is that true?"

Ellie wiped her face. "They played poker once a week."

"According to two other men we spoke to, Harold owed Fred a lot of money."

Ellie shrugged. "I don't know? Harold never told me."

"I'll need to look at your bank statements."

Ellie nodded. "Please don't hurt him."

"We hope to catch him without using force."

"Thanks, Sergeant. Uh...is that all? I need to get home."

"Try not to worry, Ellie. Things will work out."

Ellie Brockhurst had to use the windshield wipers on full to find her way home, as the rain waterfalled down. She could have used wipers for her face, too.

Chapter 15

Harold Brockhurst sat up so quickly it was like he'd been poked with a hot iron. Barking. He could hear dogs barking in the distance. He'd fallen asleep in the relative comfort of the cabin's clammy environment and was now in danger of being apprehended. Grabbing his damp clothes from the line, he reluctantly put them on. When he was all dressed and his pack loaded with the usual items, plus some non-perishable food he discovered in the cupboards, he dashed outside.

It was still raining. He shivered and set out following a trail leading up Spirit Mountain. It was probably a deer trail that had been adopted by local hunters looking for those deer. As the wet bushes rubbed against him, he felt like he was in a car wash, without the car. The trail was muddy and he had to be extra careful on the slippery rocks and roots. Where was he going? What was he going to do when he got...wherever?

He stopped after a half hour of hard breathing. He could feel the heartbeat in his temples, and sweat mixed with rain washed his face. But he could no longer hear the dogs. He noticed a clear cut ahead with piles of dead trees littering the mountain side. Maybe temporary shelter from this insufferable rain.

**

Sergeant MacFarlane tipped water off the brim of his hat. "Well keep your eyes peeled, Gus. Harold Brockhurst is a desperate man."

"But you don't honestly think he's a killer, do you?"

"Don't know...don't like to think so. But right now he's a runaway prisoner. That doesn't make him look innocent."

Three other officers were scouting the nearby cabins. They each had a German shepherd on a leash. One of them approached, "Should we move up the mountain," he said gesturing with his head.

Sergeant MacFarlane peeked up from under his hat at the blanket of grey sky. "No. Not much point, Charlie. Rain's probably washed away all tracks and scent. And I'm shriveling up like a prune. Let's call it a day."

"Here comes the boat, Sarge," said Charlie.

A Zodiac boat with police insignia on the pontoons splashed up the beach until it was high and dry. Two policemen dressed in dripping wet suits jumped over the side, each carrying a nylon duffel bag with their belongings. They clambered up the beach, seemingly in a hurry.

Doing some fishing, Sarge?" asked Gus.

"No, I had a couple of divers looking for that missing rifle as evidence. Or if there is something out there according to Harold's story."

"You boys got the right outfits for this weather," yelled Sergeant MacFarlane.

But his smile quickly vanished when one of the men suddenly bent over and vomited.

"Hey, he swallow too much water, or what Frank?" asked Sergeant MacFarlane.

"We were in the water for maybe ten minutes when Jim started floating erratically. When I grabbed him his eyes were like saucers. He kept pointing below him, but I couldn't see anything. He shook his head, pushed me away and swam for the surface." said the diver named Frank. "When we made the surface Jim says he saw something down there. Something big and black."

Jim stopped vomiting, took one step and fell.

Sergeant MacFarlane rushed to help. Jim was unconscious and seemed to have a fever, despite just coming out of the cold water. "We better get him into emergency. Gus can you keep an eye on the Zodiac for me." He threw Gus the keys. "Just in case you need to move it."

They got Jim into the rear of the police cruiser, and sped back to town.

***

"Frère a Jacques, frère a Jacques, dormez-vous, dormez-vous,"sang Frenchie.

"Ah come on Frenchie. We don't know the words to that one," moaned Cat.

"...dormez-vous, dormez-vous. Well you're supposed to learn it for French."

"Oh, no. French?" said Robert.

"Yeah," said Cat. "We get French three times a week."

"We didn't have French at my old school."

"Don't worry. Frenchie will help you. He helps me all the time."

Frenchie smiled, "Yeah you will probably catch on better than, Cat. His marks are going down because he doesn't practice."

Cat punched him on the shoulder. "Hey!"

"Yep he's goin' down. Na na na na, na na na na, hey,hey goodbye," belted out Frenchie.

Robert laughed and joined in," Na na na na, na na na na, hey hey, goodbye."

Cat joined in and soon even grandma was chanting the chorus they practiced at hockey games they attended.

"Hey look." Robert pointed out the windshield. They all stopped their singing as three police cars zoomed by.

"Wow. I wonder what's their hurry?" said Robert.

"You think they found Mr. Brockhurst?" asked Frenchie.

They fell silent thinking of poor Gilda.

***

Gilda had paced the living room so much it was a wonder there wasn't a path worn through the carpet. Thinking of her dad out in that miserable weather scared her.

It was about a half hour after the boys had dropped her off, that her mom pulled into the yard. Chester met her at the door licking at her wet pants and shoes.

"Where have you been, mom? I was worried," said Gilda.

After explaining her visit with Sergeant MacFarlane, Mrs. Brockhurst hugged Gilda.

At supper Gilda poked at the chicken, but didn't eat.

"Come on Gilda, it's 'Shake and Bake', your favourite."

Gilda shook her head. "I can't eat while dad is out there somewhere, eating crackers and cheese. Wet crackers and cheese."

"So that's where all my cheese and crackers went."

"Well it's all I could find."

"I know, dear. Don't worry. Your dad will be okay." Just then the phone rang and Mrs. Brockhurst went to answer.

Gilda stared at her chicken and had an idea.

Chapter 16

The swishing windshield wipers rhythmically cleared the soundless raindrops. Since passing the police cars the van remained silent. It had been ten minutes since they passed Gus' cabin. They were on a narrow gravel road that ran parallel to Cultus Lake. The road led to a grassy plot with an A-frame building facing the lake. Its cedar shingles were a latticework of green moss. Grey cedar siding and peeling window frames revealed the cabin's old age.

"Here we be," said Grandma.

The screen door opened and a short dark skinned old man waved.

"Hello Grandpa," said Robert, quickly climbing the stairs to the shelter of the porch. Robert bent down to hug him.

"Hello my little man," boomed his deep voice. Robert stood up straight. "What happened to my little man? You must be eating much grizzly bear, my boy, to grow so much."

"Grandpa, these are my friends Cat and Frenchie."

The old man frowned as he shook their hands. "Now those are some interesting names. There's a story behind them, I'm certain."

Robert explained, after which the old man nodded. "Names well chosen. Everything has a name, some not so well chosen. Take my wife's name, "Wise Owl".

Grandma cackled, "Ha,ha,ha. You very funny... shorty. Come on everyone let's go inside before the rain shrinks this old man anymore."

A stone fireplace stood against the far wall. A cozy fire radiated warmth throughout the large room. This room was the kitchen, and living room. A small room off to the side was the bathroom, and a set of stairs led to the bedrooms upstairs. Framed pictures covered the log walls. They were everywhere. Cat and Frenchie stood with their heads on swivels, trying to take in all the pictures of people and scenery.

"My Grandpa likes to take pictures. He says it's part of honoring his family and Mother Nature to display them.

"Cool," said Frenchie, pointing at a large photo of a grizzly bear standing on its hind legs, snarling.

"Grandpa took that one the day he forgot his rifle."

"Sacre bleu, "said Frenchie. What happened?"

"Well, I waited to see what he wanted," said Grandpa. "Was he mad at me for being there? Or was he happy to see fresh meat? Then I took his picture. He got down and walked away. It was as if he just wanted me to know whose land it really was. And the photo was proof for me to remember that."

While Cat listened, he spotted another photo, just as large but with no person or animal in it. "Is this Cultus Lake?" he asked.

Robert nodded.

"But there's nobody in this picture, it's just water."

"Take a closer look."

Cat stepped closer and studied the photo.

"Look at the water closely," said the old man.

Squinting, Cat suddenly saw, in one corner, a large dark shadow just beneath the water.

Frenchie spotted it too. His stomach clenched.

"Slalakum," uttered the old man.

Robert told us something about that, an Indian legend," said Cat.

"Tell them the story, grandpa. The legend of the Slalakum."

"Come have a seat near the fire," said the old man.

The rain continued to pelt the roof. Little natural light entered the room. The firelight cast shadows creating an eerie mood, like they were sitting in an ancient aboriginal longhouse listening to an elder recount ancestral stories.

"Our ancestors believed that Cultus Lake was the home of Slalakums. Evil spirits. The tale tells of a young Sto:lo boy who was of the age when he would become a man. Seeking his guardian spirit, he paddled out on Cultus Lake. Wearing pierced buckskin, he lifted a large rock from the bottom of the canoe, clutched it to his chest and jumped overboard. Naturally he sank. When he reached the bottom, he landed on a Slalakum roof. The Slalakum all came out to see what was the matter. Finding the boy, they took him inside. The boy witnessed a number of them were sick. They told him it was from him and others who spat into the lake. This contaminated the water. Feeling bad, the boy was able to cure the sick by rubbing away the spittle and ash from fires too close to the lake. After cleansing them, the Slalakum gave him a Tluke'l, a long icicle shaped stick. He stayed with them for a while. On returning to his village, the boy found his people would get sick at the mere sight of him. So he used the Tluke'l to heal them. In fact after that when anyone saw a Slalakum and got sick, they went to the boy who could heal them."

Only the sound of the crackling fire permeated the shadows. The tale and fire were mesmerizing.

Cat looked over at a spellbound Frenchie. "Sacre bleu. Do you think that's how you got sick that day? You saw the Slalakum?"

Frenchie gulped and shrugged.

"You saw the Slalakum?" asked the old man.

Cat told him about their fishing trip to Cultus Lake and how Frenchie said he saw something huge and black in the water. Then he got sick.

The old man nodded. Slowly he ambled over to the fireplace. From the mantle he took down a carved wooden cedar box. "This box and its contents was given to me by my grandfather, who got it from his grandfather, who got it from his grandfather, who got it...well you see this has been passed down for several generations. Some say since the legend began. Come see, boys."

The old man pointed to the lid with an eagle carving painted in red and black. "This I will pass on to Robert when I travel the trails in the next life." He opened the lid. The three boys crowded closer and gazed inside. Among crystals and rocks of many colors and sizes, he pulled out a thin icicle-shaped piece of stone, about three centimeters long. It was attached to a loop of hide, so that it could be worn around the neck.

He held it out to Frenchie. "Here, son. This is for you. For one who has seen the Slalakum." He put it over Frenchie's head. "This too is a Tluke'l, like the boy in the story had. This will protect you from the Slalakum influence. It will keep you safe from them."

Frenchie felt his face redden. "Sacre bleu. Merci beaucoup. Super! I mean thanks a lot. Cool!"

Suddenly the room burst into light. Grandma stood by the light switch on the wall. "We do have electricity, old man," she cajoled. "Snacks anyone?"

***

Climbing over the slippery dead trees, Mr. Brockhurst noticed a massive rock outcrop about fifty feet higher up the mountain. There seemed to be a dark depression that might be a cave.

He gingerly crossed the talus slope below the opening. The entrance was tall enough for him to walk into. The cave was cool inside, but a pleasant relief from the rain. He shook as much water off his wet clothes as possible. He could see only a short distance inside, so he took out his lighter and flicked it on. The floor was smooth, worn down as if it had been used a lot. It got colder the farther he went, so he stopped. He turned off the lighter to save on fuel. In the dim light from the entrance, he looked for a place to sit. There was a wide ledge of rock on one side wall. He took off his pack and sat. Stretching out his legs, he groaned. Rock chairs were not the same as Lazy Boy recliners. Suddenly the cave went dark. Something was blocking the light.

Chapter 17

"We'd better go home now," said Frenchie, looking at the clock on the wall. They'd had homemade cookies and hot chocolate while playing a game of Parcheesi with Robert's grandma and grandpa.

"I'll give you a lift, boys," said Grandma. It's a long ways to ride your bikes, especially in the rain. Robert, you get supper ready. I'll be back in forty-five minutes."

Grandma set the windshield wipers on high. They squeaked on the up strokes when the vision of a blurry road had cleared. "I can't believe all this rain." She leaned over the steering wheel, squinting.

Frenchie tapped Cat on the shoulder and pointed out his side window. The lake had white caps stirred up by the wind. "I wouldn't want to be out there today," he said.

Heavy dark clouds blanketed the sun, making it seem like dusk. As they drove past Gus' cabin, they noticed the water splashing over the dock. A light peeked out of Gus' back window.

Grandma pointed the van down the center white line. Fog now enveloped the van so she couldn't see anything beyond ten feet. If she could have seen ahead, she would have stopped. Because they were approaching the bridge, and it was gone.

***

Gilda pulled the pillow from the pillow case and replaced it at the head of her bed. She pulled the blanket off to take as well. Then she pulled the quilt back over top the mattress. She placed the items she'd taken from the kitchen, while her mom was busy on the phone, inside the pillowcase; the 'Shake and Bake' chicken wrapped in Saran wrap, a loaf of bread, a dozen frozen wieners and a package of frozen peas. She topped it off with a couple of apples and oranges. She hefted the pillow case. It was getting heavy. She would have to take her bike, even though she didn't like the thought of riding on the train tracks. The pillow case of stuff would fit in her basket.

Gilda put on another T-shirt over the one she was already wearing, a sweater and two pairs of socks. She wiped her brow. It was hot now but out in the damp air it would feel a lot colder. Especially with the steady rain.

As she descended the stairs, she could hear her mom still on the phone in the kitchen. Quietly, she took her raincoat from the closet near the front door and her mom's umbrella. Chester, who had heard her getting ready to go out, noisily paced the floor.

"Sh-sh-sh," she whispered.

His wagging tail knocked the umbrella over. Gilda looked towards the kitchen but could still hear her mom on the phone.

"Sh-sh-sh, sit boy, sit."

Chester sat but started to moan. He knew a walk when he saw one. And he certainly wasn't about to miss out on any outdoor excursions.

"Okay, okay. You can come along. But be quiet." She carefully opened the door, picked up the bulging pillow case and umbrella, and followed Chester outside.

She popped up the umbrella and quickly jogged to the barn to get her bike. She fit the pillow case of stuff into her basket carrier attached to the handlebars. She closed the barn door and rode up her driveway with Chester running along side.

When she rode past Robert's place, formerly the Beaton farm, she noticed it appeared nobody was home. The boys would have gone with Robert's grandmother to Cultus Lake. She turned off the road and aimed her bike down the center of the tracks. Her father had gone this way. As her bike bounced along the ties, she could picture him leaning into the rain with her small backpack high on his shoulders. Gilda wondered if he was he scared? Why hadn't he just stayed in jail? At least he'd had food and was dry. He was innocent, she was sure of that. How was he going to prove his innocence by running away? Maybe she could convince him to come home. Home. Her mom was probably wondering where she'd gone by now. She'd probably called the police. Whatever the case, she needed to find her father before they did.

***

Grandma screamed and yanked on the steering wheel as the van came to the edge of Thuwelman River. But the soft shoulder of gravel buckled. The van slipped over the side and tipped. The momentum caused it to roll over sideways, landing on its wheels in the fast flowing water. It floated a few feet and then the rear end got caught up in the wreckage of the bridge.

Cat groaned. He felt the seatbelt digging into his chest. His ribs hurt. Looking into the front, he saw Grandma. She wasn't moving. Her head was resting on the steering wheel. It almost looked like she was sleeping, except her face was bleeding. Tiny bits of glass showered her head. The windshield was missing. It was strange to see water coming in as the van leaned frontward. He felt for his seatbelt release and popped it open.

"Sacre bleu," said Frenchie, releasing his seatbelt. "What happened?"

"The river must have washed the bridge away," said Cat. "Grandma? Grandma are you okay?" There was no answer.

Frenchie looked out his window. "Geez, Cat. We're on the river!"

"And pretty soon we'll be in the river. Come on. We've got to help Grandma."

Cat climbed over the seat. He picked up Grandma's arm and felt for a pulse, just like he learned in the First Aid course he took at the hospital where his mom worked. Grandma had a pulse. Now what? He wished his nurse mom was here now. What would she do? Stop the bleeding. Carefully he picked off bits of glass form Grandma's face. Just then the van shifted and the water poured in over his lap.

Frenchie looked out his side. "Cat, the bridge is shifting. Looks like it will break loose soon, very soon."

Cat took out his handkerchief and swabbed the blood. It wasn't as bad as it looked. Tiny cuts from shattered glass, but nothing deep. He reached around and undid Grandma's seatbelt, then pulled her to the middle of the bench seat.

"Frenchie we will have to get out the back. You pull on her arms and I'll push. Together they got her into the back seat. Frenchie pulled the door release but couldn't open the door. He tried the other side, but couldn't open the door with the water pushing against it.

"We'll have to either go through the front and swim for it, or go out the back."

Frenchie didn't hesitate. First he climbed over the front seat, found the rear hatch release and pulled it. He climbed back over the front seat into the very back on top of the bikes. There was no way he was going in that water if he didn't have to. He managed to push the rear hatch door open with no problem. He was relieved to see the end of the bridge hung up on the bank, creating a path to the shore. The van shifted again. The bridge wreckage had created a dam and as the water rose it provided more force, threatening to push the 'bridge dam' downstream at any minute. Frenchie threw the bikes out.

"Come on Cat. She's gonna let loose at any minute." Frenchie grabbed Grandma's legs and Cat had her upper torso so they could lift and drag her out the back of the van. Luckily, she was small and relatively light. As Frenchie took one step onto shore, the whole wreckage let go.

He pulled grandma onto shore and fell backwards. When he sat up, Cat was floating away on the swift flowing Thuwelman River.

Chapter 18

Cat fell backwards on to the bridge as it floated off. He quickly got up, watching the shore and Frenchie move farther away. Like a huge raft, the bridge wreckage drifted downstream. Cat had no control. He could only watch, bound to go wherever the river took him. He could see tips of rocks poking the surface, and he knew their solid bulky mass was hidden under the waves, like icebergs that would destroy anything that came too close. He was at the mercy of the raging river.

Frenchie gulped. Geez, Cat hold on, he thought. When Cat disappeared around a corner, Frenchie regained his senses. He knelt beside Grandma. She was breathing but still unconscious. The cuts on her face had stopped bleeding. He took off his jacket and covered her as the rain persisted. Then it dawned on him, his cell phone. Why hadn't he thought of this before? He hunched over the phone taken from his jacket pocket and dialed home. But the display registered no service. He knew that some places would be out of range and possibly Spirit Mountain was blocking the signal. Now what? He had to get help for Grandma. He grabbed Grandma under her arms and began to drag her to the protection of some nearby trees. After only a couple of minutes of trying, he was huffing and puffing. It had been much easier with Cat. About another fifty feet. It was probably the hardest work Frenchie ever had to do, but eventually he dragged Grandma under some young cedar trees. It was damp under them, but it was better than being out in the open.

Gus' cabin was about two kilometers back down the road. He wished he'd had his bike, but it was on that 'raft' with Cat. They hadn't had time to move them. He was going to have to hike up to Gus' place for help. And he was already tired.

Frenchie trotted down the gravel road. He'd never been a jogger, sprinter or any kind of runner. He hated running. He usually rode his bike or got a ride from his mom. In gym class he was popular because of his personality, and the fact his best buddy was the best athlete in school. Otherwise his poor athletic ability would have seen him as always the last one picked to be on a team.

But now Cat was not there to coax him on, to get him to move his butt. He'd gone maybe half a kilometer and already he wanted to stop. But in his mind he pictured Grandma, lying there injured and Cat saying, "Come on Frenchie. You can do it."

He felt a momentary surge of adrenaline. His feet seemed lighter. After another half kilometer, he was forced to stop. He couldn't breathe in fast enough. He thought he would see his heart pop out of his chest. "Halfway there," he puffed.

The rain actually felt good on his hot face. After five minutes he started to jog again and he surprised himself that it kind of seemed easier. He told himself that if he ever got home, he'd get in better shape.

Frenchie was so glad when he ran up Gus' driveway he pumped the air with one fist and yelled "Yeah!" Well it wasn't really much of a yell, more of a gasp. But inside it felt like a yell.

He knocked on the back door. The back door creaked open. Gus looked down at Frenchie in disbelief. "What the heck are you doing here?" Gus never swore around kids.

"We had an accident. Puff...puff...puff. Grandma's unconscious and Cat's floating down river. Puff...puff."

"What...what are you talking about? Get in here, son. Let's get you some dry clothes."

"No. We haven't time." But Frenchie followed Gus inside, talking the whole time. Gus found Frenchie an old shirt of his to replace the wet one as well as a jacket. The clothes hung to Frenchie's knees, but at least they were dry.

Gus shook his head. "You guys sure get in some predicaments. Okay, well let's hop in the truck and go take a look."

It took about two minutes to travel back to where Frenchie had started his run. They found Grandma where Frenchie had left her. She was still unconscious. Frenchie and Gus carried her into the backseat of the cab, where Gus took Frenchie's wet jacket off her and covered her with a wool blanket he kept for emergencies.

"Nice job, Frenchie. But she looks bad."

Frenchie could tell that Grandma was much paler than when he had left her.

"She might have internal bleeding. We have to get help." Gus turned the truck and headed back as fast as was safely possible on the slippery gravel.

Frenchie took out his cell phone. "Geez... it still says no service."

"The phone lines are out as well. I tried before we left. This storm is creating quite a mess. I hope Cat is okay. I know he's a good swimmer, but the Thuwelman has a mind of her own. You know what Thuwelman means?"

Frenchie shook his head.

"Left its course. This river has flooded many times in the past. That's why they've built dikes. But Mother Nature can be hard to control if she wants to show who's boss."

Frenchie was surprised when Gus turned off the road before they reached his cabin. Instead he drove to the boat launch. "We have the R.C.M.P.

Zodiac. We can take Grandma across the lake and get help from the other side."

Frenchie's heart had slowed to normal. But when he heard the word 'we', it started to beat faster again. "Maybe I should wait here."

Gus turned off the engine. "I need you to come with me Frenchie. I can't drive the boat and take care of Robert's grandma at the same time."

Frenchie looked out on Cultus Lake. The place where just yesterday he'd seen that creature. That... that...Slalakum."

"Look, I know you had a bad time the other day on the lake, but you need to forget that. I need your help, Frenchie. Come on son, let's go."

His body was helping carry Grandma to the boat while his mind was still saying, "No!" But then he felt the pendant hanging on his chest. The Tluke'l. The object that according to Robert's grandfather would protect him from the Slalakum.

"Welcome to the Zodiac Futura Commando. Holds six people. Weighs only 265 pounds empty. Hypalon Neoprene buoyancy tubes. It's like riding on cushions. These are the same boats the Special Services use in combat. I rode one of these babies in the navy a few times," said Gus.

"I didn't know you were in the Special Services, Gus?"

They carefully laid Grandma on the rollup floorboard, Frenchie cradling her head as he sat beside her.

"Uh...well I wasn't actually in the forces; I was in transport and supply. I was responsible for maintaining these. Testing and inspecting. Actually quite a cool job."

"How did you get into driving dump trucks?"

"Yeah...well...life has its twists and turns, my boy. You'll find out."

Despite his rave about the water craft, Gus had difficulty getting it going. And even when he did, it didn't sound right. Not a good sign. But they needed to get Grandma George help as soon as possible. So they sped away from the shore.

Chapter 19

Cat sat in the middle of his 'formerly-a-bridge' raft. The structure was made of two-by-twelve fir planks bolted together. The original bridge had been built in 1950 by the army engineer corps out of Camp Chilliwack. Residents of the Cultus lake area had been saying for years that they needed a new bridge. Well now they would get one.

Meanwhile Cat used their old one for a pleasure craft. Only Cat would have had more pleasure if he was in control of the craft. The Thuwelman was roaring along. The once greenish-blue water was now muddy brown, with all the dirt it was carrying. There were no banks anymore. The river was simply flowing over the surrounding land. Blackberry bushes, shrubs of all varieties and tall grass poked the surface along the river's expanding edge. In some spots, the river connected the tops of fence posts like a dot-to-dot picture.

Cat had a choice. He could ride it out or abandon ship. He was trying to remember the Thuwelman's course. It did go past the mill in Cedarville where his dad worked. He remembered seeing it when his dad took him on a tour of the mill. He was sure to attract attention. But what about Frenchie? And Grandma? Frenchie probably needed help.

A sudden thump knocked him over. The 'raft' stopped. Water crept over the side as the structure tilted. It must be caught on a rock. In seconds his decision was made for him. He was swept off the 'raft' as it buckled from the water pressure. Totally submerged, he fought to get back to the surface. The cold water squeezed his body. With a lot of kicking and sweeping of his arms, he burst on top of the water. He emerged coughing up dirty river water. Fortunately he'd swam in the Thuwelman before. Hot summer days brought Frenchie and others to play in the river. But the water had been a lot calmer then. Now the river seemed mad. His body was being thrown forward like on a crazed roller coaster.

Instinctively he thrashed his arms and kicked his feet. The shore he was closest to was only about fifteen feet away. He could see the train bridge ahead. The river on the other side of the bridge had several boulders it had to maneuver around. They were probably under water by now, and Cat feared finding them the hard way. He had to get to shore, and soon.

There was a pool of calm water just ahead. He wind milled his arms and kicked with all of his strength. He was just about there when something struck him in the stomach. He stopped going forward. The water pressure pushed him under. This time he'd held his breath. He could see he was caught on a submerged tree limb. He tried to push off, but it was like backing against a wall. He was stuck. He couldn't get back up.

***

Gilda stopped at the head of the railway bridge. Chester kept going, then turned and came back. She'd never been across the railway bridge before. What if she fell? What if a train came? What if the bridge broke? She had a ton of reasons not to go across. And really only one reason said to cross. And that one reason was the only one that mattered. Her dad.

So she hopped on her seat and started pedaling. She was used to the bump-bump-bump of the railway ties. Only now the bumps were deeper as her tire went into the hole between ties. And in that hole she could see the river. The Thuwelman was moving fast. The dirty water roaring under her was entrancing, like gazing into a fire. It beckoned her. Her front wheel wobbled. Slipping sideways she quickly regained her balance. She tore her eyes away and looked up. Chester was at the far end of the bridge. Then he was gone. She could hear him barking. Please, Chester, stay away from the water she said to herself. She was halfway across when she heard a loud boom. The bridge vibrated slightly.

Instinctively, she stopped, straddling her bike afraid the disturbance would make her fall. She looked over the side and saw a huge pile of boards crash against the bridge abutment, then continue floating down river. If she'd looked harder and longer she might have seen Cat struggling to get ashore. But she needed to get across before something else happened. It was the longest trip of her life. She let out a big sigh of relief when her bike was back on solid ground.

"Chester. Chester?" she yelled. Where had he gone? She heard barking off to the left, towards the river. Oh, no she thought. Chester loved water. He'd been in the river many times, but not here, and not when the river was so high.

She couldn't see him from this high ground. "Chester," she yelled. His barking was louder and constant. What was up with her dog?

Gilda laid her bike down and carefully walked down the slope. Chester was up to his neck in the water.

Cat's strength was failing. The muscles in his arms felt like rubber. His legs limp noodles. He was so close. How could his body fail him now?

Suddenly he felt a different force. Something was tugging at the back of his shirt. The next thing he knew, Cat was above the water being pulled towards shore. Crawling and spitting out water, Cat fell onto his back on the gravelly shore. An enormous tongue licked his face. Dog breath is not the most pleasant smell to have to put up with, but in this case Cat could not get enough of it. He hugged Chester's big wet head.

"Cat? Oh, my God, Cat!" exclaimed Gilda. She helped him stand.

"Gilda. Am I ever glad to see you. And I'm sure glad you brought Chester."

"You must be freezing," she said. While they found shelter from the rain under some trees, Cat explained what had happened.

"So I've got to get back and help out Frenchie. But what are you doing here?"

Gilda explained her intention of taking some stuff to her dad.

"So you think your dad is up at the cabin?"

"That's where he told me he was going."

Cat was torn between going with Gilda and going back to help Frenchie. Gilda could tell. Good friends can usually tell what the other person is feeling. "That's okay Cat. Go help Frenchie. I'll be okay."

Cat rocked back and forth, thinking. "Uh...okay, Gilda. But as soon as I'm done I'll meet you up at the cabin, okay?"

Gilda nodded. She snuck back out into the rain and brought her bike over. She took out the umbrella and handed it out for him to take.

Cat smiled. "Uh...Gilda." He stood away from her and shook his body. Drops of water sprayed off his soaked frame. "I think it's too late for that."

She laughed. "Yeah I guess so." When Chester came over and shook his body from head to toe Cat started laughing too.

"Be careful," he said.

"You too."

Cat jogged to the river's edge and started back to where he had left Frenchie. Chester followed a ways, then trotted back to Gilda.

Chapter 20

Frenchie was surprised at the smooth ride of the Zodiac as it zipped across the choppy water. He chewed his lower lip as the wind blew his hair back and sucked the moisture off his face. The rain had finally stopped and the temperature was pleasantly warm. Lucky it was June otherwise this whole day so far would have been a lot worse. Being soaking wet in 25 degrees Celsius (77 degrees Fahrenheit) is much different than if it was October and 5 degrees. He wondered how Cat was making out. Hopefully he didn't have to swim the river. That would be cold. And dangerous.

Grandma's limp body lay on the floor. Her face was like a pale, gray mask. A mask Frenchie had seen before.

Three years ago Frenchie had gone with his mom and dad to visit his grandparents who lived in

Florida. The Boudreau family was rich. Real estate investment had made them wealthy, so wealthy they owned properties and land in several cities, including Miami, Florida. Frenchie's mom and dad chose to live in tiny Cedarville, the place where historically the Boudreau family had started. But his grandparents chose to live in a warmer spot, like so many retired people. Frenchie loved visiting because he usually got to go to Disney World in Orlando.

But on the last trip, things didn't go so well. In fact it was the worst time of Frenchie's life. They were picnicking on the beach the day it happened.

Frenchie went for a walk with his Grandma along the shoreline, gathering shells. They were quite a ways from their resting spot, out of sight from the others, when Grandma stopped.

"Frenchie, mon petit-fils. I think I've reached the end."

Frenchie laughed, thinking his Grandma was joking. But when he looked up into her face, he saw it change color. It was as if the white shell she was holding caused her tanned brown face to whiten, like a chameleon matching the color of its surroundings. Then she gently collapsed onto the sand.

Frenchie scrambled to her side. "Grandma? Grandma," he pleaded. He took her hand, hoping she would wake up. But her eyes stayed closed. That was the first time he'd seen that mask. The mask of death.

And now Grandma George was becoming a chameleon too. He blinked away the tears.

***

Cat wasn't cold, the running kept him warm. But it was not easy jogging in wet clothes. He should have taken some off, only he was in a hurry. He'd left Frenchie in a bind. Also, it was getting late, the sun would go down soon and then it would naturally get colder.

When he reached the spot where he'd left Frenchie and Grandma behind, he was surprised to see no sign of them. That was good. It must have meant Frenchie had gotten help, probably from Gus who was the closest. Or Robert and his grandpa. He could keep going to Gus' place, but he had a great desire to go help Gilda. His instincts told him Frenchie was okay. So he turned around and ran back.

What a day! He still couldn't believe that he'd just about drowned in the river. If Chester hadn't come along, well...

When Cat got back to the train bridge he stopped to catch a breath. Somewhere his mom and dad must be worried sick. He could run back down the tracks and be home in no time. Let them know he was okay. That's what he probably should do.

But he was sure his parents wouldn't want him to abandon a friend either. He could at least make sure Gilda was okay, and then talk her into going back. Once she found her dad and gave him that stuff, they could go home.

Cat took a deep breath and started up the path to the hunters' cabin.

***

He came out of his sad shell when the steady motor hum turned into an irregular choking noise, like a cat coughing up a hair ball. The boat slowed and Frenchie heard Gus swear. Frenchie gently lay down Grandma's head. He rose onto his knees, turning to face Gus. Gus was pushing switches and turning the key.

The sky was still overcast and somewhere the sun was going down. Looking ahead again Frenchie saw they were about halfway across Cultus Lake. But more than that, he suddenly realized where they were. In about the spot where he'd witnessed that dark creature. He gulped.

"Must have an oil leak," cursed Gus. It was then Frenchie saw the discoloration to the water. The oil slick that was polluting the water. "No, no we can't have that in the water."

"What?" said Gus.

"We have to get that out of there," said Frenchie.

"Uh...that's kinda' impossible, son."

"No. You don't understand. We can't pollute the water or else..."

Gus stopped fiddling with the engine. "Frenchie do you still have your cell phone?"

Frenchie reached into his jacket pocket and pulled it out. "Yep."

"Try phoning again."

Frenchie turned it on. "No. No service," he said, setting the phone beside him.

Gus stepped over to the port side and unstrapped a couple of paddles. Extending one to Frenchie he said, "Well looks like we'll have to be the motor."

The Zodiac lifted slightly and dropped. "Oh, no," he thought. "Too late."

"What was that?" said Gus.

"Slalakum," whispered Frenchie, taking the paddle.

Gus returned to the stern seat. "Come on, son. We best be going. It's going to be dark soon. You paddle on the left, I'll take the right."

Frenchie nodded and stuck his paddle over the side. But he only managed two strokes when the Zodiac lifted so high his paddle was out of the water. And then it dropped with a loud smack, like a whale's fin slapping a danger warning.

"Oh my God!" screamed Gus.

A huge black furry head peered over the port side. Gus had seen pictures of this beast. Old pictures on the Internet saying that it didn't exist. It was only a mythological creature like the Loch Ness Monster. The pictures called it a Sasquatch. Bigfoot. But he heard Frenchie call it something else. These were Gus' last thoughts as he dropped the paddle and slumped to the floor unconscious.

Chapter 21

As Cat hiked up the slippery narrow road, he couldn't help but think back to his adventure with the Beatons. How they'd kept him locked up in a bear trap up here. At the cabin he was now heading towards.

So he could kind of see how Gilda's father would feel locked up. And that's why he'd escaped. And despite the hard life her dad had made for her, Gilda loved him. Ever since Cat had known Gilda, he'd felt sorry for her. But he was proud of her stubborn strength. Despite the things she had to deal with, Gilda had shown the determination to make the best of things. She continued to rise above her challenges with a dignity that some grown-ups couldn't do.

As Cat stepped into the clearing, he saw the old cabin sprawled in the tall weeds like a sunken ship, weathered and forgotten. The rotting, moss covered log cabin was not inviting at all. And yet it was still used on occasion by hunters. And maybe by escaped prisoners.

He was still a good fifty feet away when he heard Chester. The deep bass barking would be scary if you didn't know him.

The door opened as he stepped onto the creaky porch step. Chester nearly knocked him over.

"Chester, down boy," said a smiling Gilda. "He's so happy to see you, and so am I. But my dad's not here."

"Well I can't let you camp alone. Especially in this place."

"What about Frenchie? Is he all right?"

Cat shrugged. "He wasn't there."

They went inside and closed the door. In the damp darkness there was a foul smell of mildew, or wet animal fur, or body sweat, or mouse droppings, or butchered game, or tobacco or all of these.

"We'll need to find a light, said Cat.

"Before you got here, I found this." Gilda held up a dusty cob-webbed kerosene lamp.

"Great, now all we need is a match."

They looked in all the cupboards and drawers but were unsuccessful.

"Now where would a hunter store his matches?"

"Probably in his pocket," said Gilda.

"True, Ke-mo-sah-bee." Cat walked over to the wood stove. Behind it was a tiny tin box hanging from the wall. He eased it off the nail and opened it. He held up a wooden match.

"Voila, as Frenchie would say."

"Do you know how to light one of these things?" asked Gilda holding up the lantern.

"Not really. We usually have propane or battery powered lamps when we're camping."

Once again Gilda surprised him. "Well have that match ready, Ke-mo-sah-bee," she said.

She opened the fuel cap and tilted the lamp slightly. A trickle of gas showed there was plenty of fuel. She closed the fuel tank and began pumping the air valve. After a half dozen pumps she resealed the valve.

"Okay, when I'm ready, light the match and hold it in this hole." She pointed to a hole in the base just below the glass housing.

"Okay light the match," she instructed.

Cat rubbed the end of the match on the striker plate of the tin box. The match fizzled but didn't catch. He pulled out another match with the same result. "These things must be as old as the cabin." When he took out another, he noticed the box was empty. "Last chance."

This time he applied more force. The match fizzled, but sparked to life. Cat started a victory dance and the flame wavered. He quickly stopped.

"Okay," said Gilda as she turned on the gas.

They heard the gas running into the glass chamber, but nothing was happening. The flame sputtered.

"No, no. Come on," encouraged Cat. The flame was coming to the end of the wood, warming Cat's fingers, threatening to burn him.

Gilda carefully pumped another shot of air and gleefully watched as the mantle glowed then burst into light.

Ow!" exclaimed Cat dropping the burning match. He quickly stepped on it. "Can't have us burning down the cabin."

They'd got the lamp going just in time. Any later and it would have been too dark to see to light it. Gilda set the lantern on the rough wooden table.

"You hungry?

Cat sat on the crude wooden bench next to the table. "Yeah, kind of."

Gilda dug into the pillowcase and pulled out two items. "Frozen peas or frozen wieners?"

Cat gave her a 'give-me-a-break' look. "I'm not that hungry."

Gilda laughed. "Actually here's some left-over chicken."

"But you brought that for your dad."

"Well, he's not here, is he?" she barked loudly.

Her sudden anger and frustration took Cat by surprise. He hung his head. "Sorry, Gilda."

She sniffed. A tear slipped out. The silence lingered for what seemed like minutes. She lifted her chin. "Sorry. I didn't mean to..."

"No. That's okay. I know how you feel."

Gilda gently sat down beside him and held out the bag of chicken. He reached in and pulled out a drumstick.

"I'll bet I know where he is." He took some generous bites.

Gilda set the bag on the table and wiped her face with her sleeve. "What?"

"Yeah, I'll bet he headed up to the cave. There's a cave just past the log jam where Frenchie and I used to hang out."

"Why would he go there?"

"Well, he probably figured this place was too obvious a hideout. I mean everyone in town now knows this place. Right?"

"Oh...yeah." Gilda had visions of the Beatons holding Cat prisoner here.

Suddenly Chester started growling.

Chapter 22

Frenchie dropped the paddle. His hands were shaking as he picked up the phone and prayed for service. He could barely punch in the numbers. He knew what it would say before the display came up. No service. No help. Frenchie was all alone.

Was panic in Frenchie's nature? Definitely. He'd been known to panic on many occasions. Who wouldn't panic given this predicament?

What happened next was explainable but not believable.

Frenchie aimed the phone at the creature and snapped a picture. He never really understood why he'd done this. For proof, he told everyone later. Shouldn't he be screaming at the top of his lungs for help? Or jumping overboard?

It was weird. A sense of calm flooded over him, like when you've taken some pain medicine that flows into your body and soothes. It allowed him to study the creature without fear.

The wrinkled, black, leathery face looked small centered on the huge head. Below the thick brow that jutted out like a gorilla's forehead, ebony eyes gleamed with a hypnotic intensity. Frenchie was mesmerized, but unlike Gus, he was conscious. He held out the Tluke'l. The creature's head tilted, much like a dog listening to its master. Frenchie could see gentleness in those eyes.

The creature shifted its attention to the body lying on the floor. It reached out a thick muscular arm and gently poked Grandma with one finger. In all the commotion, Frenchie had forgotten about her. She remained still, even after a couple more pokes. When the creature looked up, a tear tricked down its face. It nodded.

Frenchie could only watch as the creature partially climbed in the boat, causing it to tip down. Frenchie grabbed his seat to avoid falling. The creature bent down and scooped Grandma up. She looked like a limp doll snuggled in the beast's huge arms and chest.

With a sudden backward thrust, the creature plunged into the water and swam away on its back, Grandma still tucked to its chest. It was only seconds until Frenchie could no longer see them.

And then reality kicked back in and he started to panic. "Sacre bleu. It took Grandma. Oh my God. It took Grandma! What am I going to do?"

He was in the middle of Cultus Lake. It was getting so dark he only knew there was a shoreline by the twinkle of cabin lights in the distance. Frenchie climbed over the center seat to the stern where Gus still lay unconscious. Frenchie had an idea. Something from that story Robert's grandfather had told them. The boy with the Tluke'l could heal those affected by the Slalakum. Gripping the Tluke'l hanging from his neck with his left hand, he reached out and touched Gus with his right. Gus' hand was cold. The wrinkly hand, covered with dark brown liver spots, reminded Frenchie how old Gus really was. Despite his often playful spirit, Gus reminded Frenchie of his own grandfather.

"Come on, Gus. Réveille-toi, s'il te plait. Wake up. Please."

Gus did not move. Frenchie gave his arm a shake. "Hey, Gus. Come on, I need your help." The only sound was the water lapping the side of the boat as it gently rocked back and forth. A piece of the moon poked through the clouds.

Frenchie felt Gus' hand twitch. And again something unbelievable took place this night. Gus' eyes fluttered open.

"C'est un miracle," whispered Frenchie.

"You look like you've seen a ghost," croaked Gus.

"You are not going to believe what I've seen. I don't believe it." Frenchie helped Gus sit up.

"Comment allez-vous? I mean how are you?"

"Je ne sais pas. I don't know. It's the only French I remember you teaching me," he grinned. The grin died quickly when he saw Grandma was not on board. When Frenchie explained what had happened, Gus was horrified. It was the second time Frenchie heard Gus swear.

"Well what are you waiting for, pick up that paddle. We've got to get Search and Rescue out here."

Frenchie sat up front and started paddling. "Isn't this their boat?"

"Yeah, and a lot of good it did us." Then it was the third time Frenchie heard Gus swear.

Frenchie could not keep up Gus's pace, but he tried his best. For every dip of his paddle, Gus took two, sometimes three. The rain had stopped, but the starless sky suggested it could easily rain more. It had seemed like days had passed since Frenchie and Cat had pulled Grandma out of her van. Where was Cat, now? Still floating down the Thuwelman? Stuck somewhere on a river bank or hung up on rocks? Frenchie prayed he was okay.

Frenchie's shoulder was burning. He was so tired. He'd had more exercise today than he'd had all month. First doing his chores, and then riding to Robert's, that all seemed like last week now. Then the accident at the river, pulling Grandma to safety. Later running to Gus' place for help. And now paddling to shore. He would sleep for a week after this!

He was getting cold, too. Ever since the sun had gone down, the temperature continued to drop. But the lights were getting closer. Somewhere his mom must be freaking out. Wait until she found out about his day. No, he'd better not share too many details. She'd have a heart attack.

He shivered. Now he wished he had taken those mittens and toque.

"How are you doing, son?"

"I feel like I could sleep right here in the boat." That's when he felt the bottom scraping on sand. They floated partly up the beach and Gus jumped in. Up to his knees he grabbed the bow rope and pulled. Frenchie jumped out and helped pull, even though his arms felt like limp noodles. They pulled the Zodiac as far as they could.

The silence was broken by a ringing. Not just any ringing, but a tinny version of 'Hockey Night in Canada'.

Frenchie pulled the cell phone from his front pocket. Service. At last! He pushed the talk button.

"Hello?"

Chapter 23

Chester was standing staring at the door. Every once in a while he cocked his head as if trying to listen better.

"Probably just a squirrel," said Cat.

Gilda gulped and nodded.

Chester sniffed at the door quite a few times, then sneezed so loudly it made Gilda jump.

Cat chuckled, "Too many different smells for him, must be clogging up the old snout."

Chester circled a few times, and then lay down.

"Well at least we have a guard at the door," said Cat. The lantern flickered briefly, and then burst back to full light. "I don't know how long that thing will burn. We should probably try and get some sleep."

There was a wooden bunk bed tucked against the far wall. "Do you want the top or bottom?" asked Cat.

"Uh...are there any mice in here do you think?"

"Little field mice, yeah, could be but..."

"Then I'll take the top," said Gilda.

Cat couldn't believe tough old Gilda who would stand up to kids twice her size would be afraid of mice. He stared at her.

"What?" she exclaimed, climbing up the flimsy ladder. "I just don't like mice, okay." When she plopped down on the mattress, a cloud of dust burst into the air.

"And you are leaving your boots on to stomp on them?"said Cat with a smirk on his face.

Gilda smiled, "Never know when you might have to make a quick exit."

"Well don't stomp on me on the way down," he joked. Cat slipped off his boots and pulled up the grey wool blanket. He was glad the lighting was poor so he couldn't see the mattress. Who knows what condition it was in? He climbed on top and lay back. It was like lying on a board with a rock for a pillow. But despite the discomfort, he was asleep in minutes.

Gilda on the other hand could not sleep. And it was not her fear of mice. Although she thought she heard scratching or chewing noises. She remembered her first mouse encounter. She was three years old at the time. Her mom and dad dropped her off at a babysitters. The young girl babysitter was good to Gilda. Unfortunately the girl was in charge of looking after her five year old brother as well. He had a pet mouse. When the sitter wasn't paying attention, the boy put the mouse in Gilda's pajamas. She screamed and cried as the mouse scrambled all over her looking for a way out. Even after the girl got the mouse out, Gilda sobbed until her parents arrived.

No it wasn't mice she was thinking about. It was her dad of course. She would not stop worrying until he was safe. Even if he had to go back to jail. She thought about taking the lantern and going to find him. But, no, she wasn't that brave. If the light should go out, as it surely would at some point, she'd be in the dark, alone. She could easily get lost.

Then she thought about how her mom was probably worrying now too. Maybe she should not have come. She wasn't able to help her dad so far. She hadn't even seen him. All of these worries stuck in her head and she couldn't dismiss them. It was like getting chewing gum stuck in your fingers. Just when you get one little piece pulled off it sticks to your other hand. But sleep finally did overtake her after hours of staring at the shadows flickering in the lantern's light.

Cat walked over and picked up the lantern. He stepped over a sleeping Chester, opened the door and exited. The sun was just coming up and the grass and shrubs glistened with dew. He stepped off the porch. As soon as his feet touched the cold damp earth, he realized he'd forgotten to put on his boots. He set the lantern down. It was then he noticed it.

A towering figure, as dark as coal and as hairy as a musk ox stood on two feet at the edge of the meadow. It reminded Cat of what Frenchie had seen. It reminded him of what Robert's grandfather had talked about. What was it called again? Oh, yeah. Slalakum. And it was holding something next to its chest. No, not something, someone. Cat froze. He was scared.

The creature must have seen him. It stepped out of the clearing and went back into the forest. Cat snapped out of his trance and ran after it. He needed to see who the creature had taken. "No, stop," he yelled. As if the creature would do his bidding, let alone understand him.

When he reached the edge of the woods, he could see no sign of it. Nor would he ever be able to, unless the creature wanted to be seen. It had vanished into the forests of Spirit Mountain.

***

Cat felt something wet probing between his toes. It tickled and he moved his leg. Then he felt something wet and warm caressing his face. He opened his eyes and saw Chester staring at him. He appeared to be grinning as his mouth hung open and his long pink tongue dangled to one side.

"Ouuuu, dog breath." He gently pushed Chester away and sat up.

Light filtered in through the dirty cobwebbed window over the sink. Cat swung his legs over the side of the bunk, noticing how dirty his socks were. They felt damp and the smell was...well, bad. He quickly put his boots on. He stood and saw Gilda stretching on the top bunk. Her eyes fluttered open.

"Hey, Ke-mo-sah-bee. It's a new day. We got things to do, people to meet, so get up slow poke, on your feet," announced Cat.

Gilda yawned. She couldn't believe she'd actually fallen sleep. "Yeah, yeah, yeah."

"Sorry, just a poem my dad uses on me sometimes."

Gilda slowly climbed down the ladder. Chester greeted her with wagging tail and face licks.

"I had the weirdest dream last night," said Cat. "I saw this creature, a Slalakum, Robert calls it, and I followed it to the edge of the woods. It disappeared. But it was carrying someone."

"Someone?"

"Yeah. Weird, hey?"

"Where's the lantern?" asked Gilda.

Cat stared at the table. No lantern. Cat looked around for it.

Meanwhile Gilda took the bread from her pack, broke off a hunk and gave it to him. It was a little hard but he chewed with gusto and was quickly done. He walked over and opened the door. Chester seized the opportunity to dash to the nearest bush.

Cat scooped water with his hands from the rain barrel just on the open side of the porch. That's when he saw it. The lantern sat on the bottom step of the porch.

When Gilda came out for a drink, he pointed at it.

"Maybe you weren't dreaming," she said.

Chapter 24

"Maybe we should go home," said Cat.

"But we've come this far," said Gilda. "I want to find my dad."

"But that creature is out there, somewhere."

"I don't care." She pet Chester's head. "Besides I have Chester here to protect me, right boy?" Chester, hearing his name, looked up at her and barked.

"Somehow I don't think that'll be enough, no offense, Chester." Chester barked again.

"Well, I'm going. You coming?" Gilda swung the half empty pillowcase over her shoulder and started up the trail.

Cat shook his head but followed.

Chester took the lead, but relinquished it now and then to sniff certain bushes. He'd catch up to them, and then race on ahead. The trail was easy to follow, being used by hikers, hunters, trail bikers, and wildlife. It climbed steeply through second generation forests of mostly deciduous trees. Remnants of clear cut logging still clung to the slopes like the tidal debris left behind by an ocean. Only this was man made, not an environmental occurrence. Logging at that time was not ecologically motivated.

After an hour of hiking, they came to an area known as the log jam. They had to climb over piles of logs that had been just left there to rot. Tiny evergreens poked through spots hoping to reestablish the forest.

Cat stopped to catch his breath, Gilda right next to him. Standing on top of the pile, he looked down on the scenery below. He'd been here several times, but it always looked spectacular. The multi-greens of the forest melted into the patchwork yellows, browns and greens of rectangular fields of all shapes and sizes in the flat river valley. Snaking through this mosaic was the Thuwelman River, twisting and turning in its journey to the Pacific a hundred kilometers west. Even from this distance Cat could tell the Thuwelman was spilling its banks, like an engorged boa constrictor shedding its skin in order to grow. Several fields were flooded. He could see the tiny blue square that was his home. Fortunately it was far enough away from the river so it wouldn't be flooded. He wondered what his parents were doing. Probably on the phone trying to locate him.

Off to the right, out of sight, was Cultus Lake. Cat wondered what Frenchie was up to? And how was Grandma?

Chester's barking disturbed his reverie. He watched Chester weave through the logs and lope up the mountain, his nose to the ground.

"He's got a scent," said Gilda.

"Yeah. I hope it's a friendly one. He's headed to the cave," said Cat. "It's between those rocks up there that form a V-shape."

Nimbly, they climbed off the pile and hiked over the talus slope, trying to catch up to Chester.

"Chester, wait up," pleaded Gilda.

They could only watch as Chester disappeared inside the cave.

"I hope the owner of that cave is not home," said Cat. Although he'd been inside, he always wondered if anything lived there on a more permanent basis. Besides squirrels, field mice or the odd bird that is. He was hoping not to find any large mammals in there.

Breathing hard, they both stared into the gloom. A moaning, whining sound emerged.

Cat jumped when Chester suddenly popped out the four foot high hole. The dog whined, poked his snout at Gilda's legs, then whined some more.

"What's up, boy?" she asked.

Chester ran back inside.

"I think he wants us to follow," said Gilda.

"I wish we had that lantern, fuel and matches."

Gilda raised her forefinger. She dug into her pillowcase and pulled out a candle and a package of matches. "Voila," she said victoriously.

"Where did you get those?"

"I found them during the night on the top bunk. There was a little shelf with some 'reading material' and these things. I guess someone liked to read up there. Well, actually, mostly look at disgusting pictures.

Cat took the package of matches. 'Betty's Café' was printed on the cover. "Hey this is from Cedarville, only now it's a 'Pizza Hut'. I hope the matches still work."

Cat opened the package, pulled a match off the tab and struck it against the rough strip on the back. It popped into flame. Carefully, he held it to the candle wick until it flared.

"Okay. Here I go."

"I'm right behind you."

After the narrow entrance, the cave widened enough for them to stand up. The black rock walls glistened with dampness; bands of a white crystalline mineral zigzagged at various intervals. There was a musky smell. The floor was the same dark rock. Carefully they inched their way along, the flickering candle casting shadows around them.

Chester had disappeared ahead somewhere and soon renewed his whining.

About twenty feet inside they stopped. Chester was sitting beside something lying at his feet. It looked like a pile of clothes, until Cat raised the candle slightly. They saw a head. A human head. Gilda's father's head.

"Dad!" she exclaimed, rushing past Cat. She flew herself down and lifted his head. He was unconscious but breathing.

"Oh, dad. I love you," she said, cradling his head in her arms.

Cat knelt beside her, holding the candle closer to Mr. Brockhurst's face. "He looks awfully pale."

Gilda checked over her father's body. "I don't see any wounds."

"Maybe he hit his head." They checked his head but found no bumps or bruises.

Cat shone the candle around looking for any evidence as to what might have happened. "Hey, look." He pointed a finger to the opposite wall. He crossed to the opposite side and picked up what he had spotted. A rifle. A rifle with the barrel bent completely backwards. He carried it over to show Gilda.

"Sacre ble," she whispered. "What happened to that?"

"I've go a feeling your dad had a visitor."

"What? What are you talking about?"

"I think I know what happened to that rifle and what might be wrong with your dad."

Chapter 25

"Slalakum?" asked Gilda.

Cat nodded. "The same thing happened to Frenchie. Just seeing one can cause people to become sick, sometimes go unconscious."

"We've got to get help."

"Well we can't carry your dad down the mountain, that's for sure. I'll go for help while you take care of him."

Gilda chewed on her bottom lip. "But what if that thing, that Slalakum comes back?"

"I know this might sound weird, but I don't think they are dangerous. I mean sure they make you sick and cause you to black out, but they don't actually hurt you. I think that's just their way of defending themselves."

"You're right. That does sound weird." Gilda gazed down at her dad's face. "Okay, go. But please hurry."

"I'll leave you the candle and matches." He pointed to Chester asleep by the entrance. "And you've got a guard."

A loud snore came from Chester. "Yeah, some guard," joked Gilda.

Cat laughed. "Hey, he's had a busy few days. See you in a while."

As he stepped out of the dark, he had to cover his eyes momentarily from the bright sun. His stomach growled. Although he was missing his breakfast, he didn't have time to dwell on it. He scampered over the log pile like a sure-footed mountain goat. He always found going down the mountain a breeze. It took him less than half the time it took going up. When he reached the hunters' cabin, he took a quick look around to see if anyone might be there. He knew there was probably a search team out by now. But the cabin was empty, so he quickly scooted down the trail as fast as he could without slipping on rocks or roots.

When he reached the bottom, he slowed to a walk, catching his breath. The closest help would be at Gus' cabin, if he was home. The next closest would be Robert's grandparents' cabin. The Thuwelman River covered the trail in spots, so he had to weave around the water by finding higher ground. One such area was the 'murder site'. Yellow flagging still drooped from the trees. Cat climbed over some fallen trees at the edge to get around the pond of flood water. That's when he heard something. Not just something. His name. Someone was calling him.

"William." The voice came from above. Cat stood balanced on a log and looked up. He couldn't believe it. Someone was calling him from twenty feet up an enormous cedar. The same tree where they'd found the murdered man.

Cat squinted in recognition. "Grandma?"

"Help an old lady out, would you please my boy."

The log he was standing on made the first branch within reach. Cat climbed the tree, with not too much difficulty as its branches were thick and spaced just right. It was almost like a staircase climbing the old tree. He found Grandma wrapped to the tree with some kind of twine.

"Grandma, you're okay?" he said with uncertainty.

"Well I've slept in better places. Can you help me get out of this stuff?"

It took a lot of twisting and unraveling to free her from the strong cords. As soon as he pulled off the last strand, she gave him a big hug. Just then they heard voices. Cat recognized one immediately.

"Gus!" he yelled.

The voices stopped and Cat saw several people come into the clearing, edging around the pool of water.

"William?" called Gus.

"Up here," Cat shouted.

Gus appeared under them. "What in the devil are you doing up there?"

"It's a long story. An unbelievable story."

***

Gilda watched the candle flame getting smaller and smaller. Finally it was so small it was just a dot.

In a few seconds it was going to be completely dark. Cat had only been gone for maybe an hour. But it seemed like she'd spent a whole day waiting.

Suddenly Chester barked. Gilda jumped. "What is it?"

He ran out of the cave.

As the light died, she felt colder. A shiver ran up her spine. In the dark, her mind was free to imagine the worst. What was out there? The Slalakum? Had it come back? Would she get sick and pass out?

She heard Chester's bark in the distance. Then he stopped and it got quiet for a long time. When she heard something moving towards her, her heart started racing. Something cold, moist and hairy touched her hand. She recognized it instantly.

"Hi Chester. Good boy."

A light flashed inside. Gilda breathed a huge sigh of relief when she heard someone call her name.

Chapter 26

The hospital room was finally quiet, as only Gilda, Frenchie and Cat stood over the patient. Police, nurses and other adults had left them alone for the time being. One officer sat outside.

Gilda picked up her dad's hand. It felt cold. She'd overheard the nurse tell her mom the doctors did not know what to do. He was getting weaker and weaker, despite the medications they'd given.

"Okay Frenchie. Have you got it?" asked Cat.

Frenchie pulled the Tluke'l out from his shirt where it hung around his neck and held it up.

"That's it?"questioned Gilda.

"Yep. I know. It doesn't look like much, but it worked on the policeman." Cat explained how Frenchie had just come from police officer Jim's room. He too had been unconscious. When Frenchie held the man's hand and displayed the

Tluke'l, the officer came to as if he'd only been asleep. The nurses were stupefied.

"Well give it a try then," said Gilda anxiously. Frenchie took Gilda's dad's hand away from her, while she looked hopefully at her dad's face. Several minutes passed. The only sound was the beeping monitor hooked up to Mr. Brockhurst. Frenchie squeezed the Tluke'l. Several minutes passed.

"It's not working," moaned Gilda.

Cat gave Frenchie a pleading look. Frenchie shrugged.

Just then the door opened. A familiar voice said, "How are my favorite grandchildren?" Grandma's tiny figure slid through the entrance like a mouse through a crack. She seemed as bubbly as usual, showing no signs of strain from her ordeals.

Cat introduced Gilda and explained what had happened to her dad.

"Oh, my. The Slalakum have been busy. I know about your dad, Gilda. They told me. You see the Slalakum have been around for as long as my people, some say longer. They choose to remain hidden, but it is getting more and more difficult to do so. They have tried to ignore those who would pollute their water and land. But sometimes they cannot overcome their natural instincts to protect their home. That is what happened to Fred, the man who was killed. After he was tipped from his boat the Slalakum tried to save him. It took his body to the big cedar. There his body was placed high in the branches away from possible predators. Just like me he was tied so he wouldn't fall. But his heart was not strong. His goodness in question."

"But my dad has a strong heart, I know he has. And he is good...I know it hasn't always been so...but he is good. Please I know he is," sobbed Gilda.

"Your father has given up his spirit. He needs to be convinced he's worthy of this life."

Gilda grabbed her dad's hand. "Listen dad. I want you back. Please wake up. You are innocent. Grandma knows. And Frenchie too."

Frenchie nodded.

Grandma stared at Mr. Brockhurst's face, as if willing her thoughts into him. "So you are free of the burden of your friend's death. He is on a better path than he was in this world. Come back to us. Come back to your daughter."

Several quiet, awkward minutes passed. Slowly, Gilda felt her father's hand getting warmer. His body quivered and then she saw his eyes flutter open.

"Oh, dad!" She hugged and kissed him.

Chapter 27

After a week, the waters of the Thuwelman receded back to normal. Much farmland had been flooded. Frenchie and Cat's houses escaped any damage, but Gilda's basement was waist deep in water.

School was closed that week, much to the happiness of all the kids. It gave them time to try out homemade boats and see how much water they could ride their bikes through.

Frenchie, Cat and Robert helped Gilda and her mom bail out their basement. This gave them time to talk about all the events that had happened. This had been one unbelievable Y-file.

Mr. Brockhurst, having fully recovered ,was in the Vancouver jail awaiting his hearing. A judge would examine the case to determine if it would go to trial.

On Saturday, the Katt, Boudreau and George families all travelled to Vancouver to be with Gilda and her mom at the hearing. As it turned out the only evidence linking Mr. Brockhurst to Fred Smith's death was the rifle. And when Mr. Brockhurst held the rifle up, with the bent barrel pointing back at him, the audience burst into laughter.

"Yes it is my rifle," he said, restraining a laugh. "I don't think I would be firing it any time soon, though." He then went on to explain how something tipped the boat, causing Fred to fire the weapon several times. "He must have shot himself somehow. I was knocked unconscious."

Grandma gave her testimony about a creature of the lake that could easily tip a boat. She told the court about the Slalakum. The silence of the courtroom was broken by whispers from the crowd.

When she'd finished, the judge thanked her for her 'evidence', but he found it far-fetched, the 'Loch Ness Monster Theory' he called it. This brought more laughter from the crowd until Frenchie stood up shouting, "But it's true."

"Please sit down, young man. You are out of order."

"I didn't know I was in line," said Frenchie. Once again the crowd broke into laughter. Mrs. Boudreau pulled him, "Sit down, Francis, and behave yourself."

As he sat back down he said, "But it's true. I have proof, mom." He pulled out a paper from his pocket and held it up.

"Well, in the interest of justice and a quiet courtroom, bring that here young man."

Frenchie straightened his glasses and slowly walked to the judge's podium. He stood on tiptoes trying to reach the judge. The bailiff took it from him and handed it to the judge.

The judge put on some glasses and examined the paper. "This is a picture of a...uh...a gorilla?"

"A Slalakum, sir."

"Oh...oh... of course, this so called Slalakum. So where did you cut this out of, son? One of those fantasy magazines?"

"No, sir. I took that with my cell phone. I still have it on there, too, if you want to see."

"That won't be necessary." The judge gave the picture to the bailiff.

"May I see?" asked Grandma still sitting in the witness box. The judge nodded.

The bailiff handed her the picture. She nodded. "The Slalakum."

In the crowd Gus sat listening to all the testimony. Like everyone else, he would not believe it either, if he hadn't seen it with his own eyes. He stood. "Your Honor, I also can bear witness to a sighting of the creature."

The crowd turned heads and were silent. They believed the boy capable of making things up. The old lady maybe seeing things that weren't there. But Gus was a well respected member of the community. A war veteran.

On the stand Gus gave his account of that day on Cultus Lake. Again, there was a lot of whispering after he'd done.

The judge knew Gus as well as anyone in Cedarville. Never a more honest man. "Well I must say this story would make a good X-file." The crowd laughed.

Cat looked at Frenchie. "Or Y-file," he whispered."

The judge continued, "But that show was cancelled years ago. I must say that there is insufficient evidence to suggest this was a crime. It would appear that whatever unknown forces were at work, this was an accident. I hereby release the suspect, Mr. Brockhurst. You are free to go." He banged his gavel and the courtroom turned into a noisy turbulence.

Gilda, with her mom close behind, pushed through the people to wrap her arms around her dad. This time he had not let her down.

Chapter 28

The next week school was back as usual. Cat gave his news report on Wednesday morning. He told about his experiences during the flood. The class and Mr. Simms were awed by his adventures.

On Friday the class presented their 'fairy tale' adaptations. When it was Cat's group's turn, Frenchie grabbed a large bag from the coat rack and joined Cat, Robert and Gilda in the hall. In the bag were various props and costume items. As narrator, Robert had a special Sto:lo necklace and cedar hat his grandpa had lent him. While the rest got ready, he went back into the room and sat on a chair at the front of the class. There were a few oohs and ahhhs at his attire, as he began, "Ou'xia, the cannibal woman meets Hansel and Gretel. Once upon a time…" Robert went on to explain the Sto:lo myth of the Slalakum known as Ou'xia.

When it was time, Cat and Gilda entered as Hansel and Gretel. Cat had shorts, long socks, a vest and an alpine hat with feather he'd borrowed from Frenchie. Gilda had her yellow spring dress and a white apron on. She was carrying a basket. Looking like two German kids out gathering strawberries, they stopped when the door reopened and in came Ou'xia. Frenchie wore a dress and a bonnet his mom had found for him, and Grandma's shawl which, because she was such a small woman, fit him nicely. The laughter in the room was so loud that Mrs. Cook at the office wondered what was going on. In a croaky voice Frenchie said, "Grandchildren. Close your eyes and open your mouths and I will give you something good to eat."

***

A temporary bridge had been installed at a different spot on the Thuwelman, closer to the landfill site, near the 'Slalakum tree' as the Y-files team called it. This was where Cat, Frenchie, Gilda and Robert had decided to meet on the first Saturday after school was done for another year.

Cat and Frenchie rode on their new bikes. Well they weren't brand new, but just about. Having lost their bikes in the flood, Sergeant MacFarlane gave them each a bike from the 'unclaimed items' warehouse. The bikes had been there over a year gathering dust. He said they had earned them for their hard work and bravery shown to Grandma George and Mr. Brockhurst.

"I wish I had lost my bike," snorted Robert, his large body hunkered over his tiny bike, his feet turning the small wheels a mile a minute trying to keep up.

Cat laughed. "I'll put in a good word for you to Sergeant MacFarlane."

When they reached the 'Slalakum tree', they lay their bikes down and found a dry spot under the huge cedar.

"Gus asked if we want go fishing next week," said Cat.

"From the dock?" asked Frenchie.

"Come on, you're still not scared to go out in the boat, are you? After all you are the holder of the Tluke'l."

"Grandma says the Slalakum are gone," said Robert.

"What?"

"Yeah. She says they have gone to find another home."

"One thing still bugs me, Frenchie. How come when you first saw the Slalakum out on the lake, you weren't sicker, like Gilda's dad or the man who died? You were unconscious for only a short time."

Robert spoke up, "My grandpa says the young are not as susceptible to the spells of the Slalakum. Their imaginations allow for the unexplained to be ...well, unexplained. They can believe in such things."

"Well can you believe in this?" said Cat holding out a picture. It was a picture of Frenchie dressed up as Ou'xia.

Frenchie said," I can't believe I did it."

Their laughter added life to the sunny day. It promised to be a great summer holiday.

LaVergne, TN USA
27 December 2010
210213LV00001B/11/P